JOBURG STEELE

GRAHAM TEMPEST

BRIGHTWAY PRESS INC.

JOBURG STEELE
A Brightway book

Brightway Press Inc.
522 Hunt Club Blvd, #316
Apopka, Florida 32703

ISBN (Print version) 978-0-9996727-2-3

JOBURG STEELE is a work of fiction.

Like the imaginary South African province of *Protea*, names, characters, places and incidents either are the product of the author's imagination or are used fictitiously and any resemblance to actual persons living or dead, businesses, companies, events or locales is entirely coincidental.

For Raficq

PROLOGUE

Watch your step!" said Rebekka nervously. She put a hand on Oliver's shoulder to steady herself.

They walked through the darkness towards her car which was parked downtown near the brooding tower of the Carlton Hotel, once a handsome symbol of South African pride but long since shuttered due to lack of business, still in place but decaying inside.

The dead hotel's brown sides, studded with sightless black windows, sloped up at a slight angle for a dozen floors before straightening and soaring vertically aloft. Down below, trash dotted the sidewalk. Shadowy people milled around, poorly dressed. Rebekka gripped her purse tighter.

"I must say I'm glad of your company," she muttered.

He shot her a glance. Wavy dark hair, good figure. Pretty. Earlier in the day she had teased him about being flippant and not expressing his feelings. Smart, too.

"So is this the *real* Joburg?" he asked.

She considered the question. "There are two Joburgs, separated by a bloody great poverty gap. One is the smart northern suburbs, including the Country Club with 35 acres of green lawns, croquet and cricket. The other looks more like this – dirtier, rougher and blacker after several decades of white flight."

"What happened to the businesses that used to be here?"

"They moved to the suburbs – the Johannesburg Stock Exchange is in Sandton now." She reached out to open the car door.

A grey flatbed truck swept out of the darkness, almost hit them and slammed into the Toyota. There was a jarring impact and the screech of metal on metal as the truck gouged a three foot furrow in the car's flank, ripped the passenger door off its hinges and shuddered to a halt.

Two minutes later the truck, carrying Rebekka, had disappeared and Oliver was lying bloodied and senseless on the concrete.

1

ONE WEEK EARLIER

The sky blue Rolls with darkened windows swished up to my house in Chelsea and breathed to a stop. A tinted pane slid down.

"Looking for Oliver Steele."

"You've found him," I said.

The chauffeur got out and opened the passenger door. A man stepped out, a short figure in a dark suit, dazzling white shirt and MCC tie, the city version with the club's monogram repeated in red and gold on a navy background.

He looked me up and down. I had been digging in my small garden and was wearing muddy jeans and a wool sweater with torn elbows. He glanced up at the white Georgian facade of my house, then back at me.

I had no idea who he was, but I waved him inside. I invited the chauffeur in too, but he shook his head and stayed outside. Probably afraid some Chelsea lowlife would key the Rolls.

"We haven't met, but it's coffee time and you look as though you have a story to tell," I said.

"I am Sir Paul Coward. Carlton Tisch gave me your name."

"Not a good start," I said, tinkering with the espresso machine.

He blinked. Watch the sarcasm, I thought, it's risky. But it gave me early warning of his lack of a sense of humour. As well as a touch of insecurity? One of those knights who like to mention the honorific. Others modestly avoid the subject; it usually comes up sooner or later anyway.

He flashed a smile that came and went. It was a diplomat's 'I believe in good manners so as not to seem rude, but I really just want to get on with things' smile.

"How do you know Carlton?" I asked.

"We sit on some boards together."

"Which ones?"

He frowned. "Several public companies."

I was not impressed. In my experience, most decisions in publicly quoted companies are made by managers, not directors. As often as not, directors are there because they are required by law. They earn too much money for turning up at occasional board meetings, uttering platitudes and going to lunch.

I took a closer look at Coward. He fit the profile. Conventionally handsome – strong cleft chin, even tan, penetrating blue eyes. Which is fine if you like being stared at penetratingly. I don't. We had not shaken hands – at least he had the sense to skip that un-British ritual –

but he probably had a firm trustworthy grip to go along with the clear-eyed gaze. A shame about his height, around five foot one, it rather spoiled the effect.

I made a *cappuccino* for myself. He accepted a *latte* and slowly stirred in six heaped spoonfuls of sugar.

His eye strayed around the small sitting room as if valuing the furniture. "He says you are available for assignments."

"Five million," I said.

"Excuse me?"

"The house, excluding contents. And rising daily. It's the location."

He nodded. I suspected he had already priced it himself. Now he was wondering how a young accountant could afford a four bedroom house in Cale Street.

"What exactly is your relationship with Mr. Tisch?" he asked.

How much had Carlton told him? That I was bankrupt, still trying to drag myself out of debt? That the house was Carlton's, who let me live there in exchange for dropping whatever I was doing and hustling over to his Tortola villa whenever a crisis arose?

Better give him something to chew on.

"I'm Carlton's financial advisor – just a common or garden bean counter really. But since starting work for him I've had to kill – strictly in self-defense, of course – a Colombian drug dealer on Guadeloupe, a Qaddafi-era thug in the Libyan desert and an Algerian terrorist in Paris."

He blinked.

"Oh, and recently a corrupt police inspector on Cayo Santa Maria. That's a pretty strip of sand just off the north coast of Cuba."

From the look on his face I don't think Carlton had told him any of that.

"That's about it. Go ahead," I said.

He pulled himself together with a start.

"I am the chairman of an international investment group. We provide money for projects to combat poverty around the world."

"I am impressed."

"Two years ago, we invested fifty million dollars to build affordable homes for poor people in South Africa."

"Very worthy."

"It's a joint venture with the government of the South African province of Protea. The province has a twenty percent stake. We have twenty percent also. The other sixty percent is supposed to be issued to the owners of the homes. Little people, in other words."

"All good by me."

He frowned. "Unfortunately, things haven't turned out that way."

"You've lost money?"

"Yes."

"That can happen."

He stared at me. "You are quite young. Carlton says you were a partner in a city firm."

"Correct."

"What happened?"

"The partnership dissolved. I'm twenty-eight."

"Where did you go to school?"

"Bunnington, then Oxford." That struck me as not particularly relevant, but it seemed to please him.

"I was at Wellington," he said.

"Good for you."

He frowned. "We need someone to go down there and find out where the money has gone."

"Okay."

"There is an audit going on but we're not getting any feedback from the auditors. Instead, we are being pressed to put in more money."

"Pressed by whom?"

"The builders, an outfit called Bosu Construction."

"That is the company that you chose?"

He appeared to consider the question. "Well I suppose that technically we did the choosing. But they came highly recommended by Tom Maputo, the finance minister of Protea."

He was looking a bit hangdog now, like someone who realises he made a serious mistake and is trying to decide whether to come clean and admit it or whether to go on producing clever excuses, deflecting blame onto anyone but himself.

"If Bosu Construction is being audited, you presumably have the right to review the auditors' findings?"

He brightened. "Yes, it's in the contract."

"What happens if you find Bosu have been cooking the books?"

"We could fire them."

"That's difficult though, right? I mean, if they are

halfway through building a bunch of houses you would
be starting again almost from scratch."

He fidgeted. "Yes."

"At great expense?"

"I suppose so."

We sipped our coffee. The silence was awkward as if,
after he had made a big effort to come all the way here,
he didn't know what to say next. I tried to help him out.

"What's the real cause of the problem?"

"I can't prove it, but I think it's the Bosu brothers."

"And exactly who are they?"

"Shiv, Haresh and Dinesh. Three scoundrels, in my
opinion."

"Indian?"

He nodded. "Shiv, the eldest, is a very smooth operator. Devious. Up to all sorts of tricks, including but not
limited to wholesale bribery and corruption."

High praise from someone like Coward. "What about
the others?"

"Dinesh, the youngest, is a nobody. But the middle
brother, Haresh, is something else. Watch out for him!"

"Meaning?"

"A bit of a maniac."

"Have you met him?"

"Briefly, when we were setting up the contracts."

"What does a maniac look like?"

"He has a glass eye and a scar across his cheek."

At first I thought he was joking, but he did not smile
so I assumed it was a simple statement of fact.

"Okay."

For a minute neither of us spoke.

"Do you have any questions?" he asked.

"No."

He frowned. "Why not?"

"You said you weren't getting feedback so I doubt if there's much more you can tell me."

I picked up the phone.

"What are you doing?" he asked.

"Calling the airlines. More coffee?"

2

"Thirty million rand for a picnic?" asked auditor Lucy Gray. "Is that a reasonable business expense?"

She adjusted the glasses on her good-natured face and smiled at thin-cheeked Dinesh Bosu.

They were sitting alone at one end of a long table in the boardroom of the Protea office of Bosu Construction. Dinesh was the company's president and, along with his two brothers, its owner.

He was the least intelligent of the brothers. He was smartly dressed – dark trousers, white shirt, gold cuff-links – but his narrow face and worried frown betrayed an anxious nature and he looked plain and undistinguished. He trailed through life in the wake of the other two, taking care of minor tasks where it wouldn't matter too much if he screwed up.

However, he was just as single minded as his

brothers in the pursuit of profit. The idea that any expense would not be allowed as a tax deduction was unthinkable. Like Lucy, he expressed the amount in South African rand, but since the family's business was nothing if not international, he mentally converted it into American dollars. The sum they were discussing was worth about two million dollars or one point six million pounds sterling.

"Some very important customers were present. Thirty million is about what we pay you in annual fees, by the way."

Lucy flushed. That was true, but it was bad form to link audit fees to this discussion.

She turned over a page in the file. "There were four hundred guests."

Bosu smirked. "It was quite an affair."

Lucy straightened her papers. She was bright and cheerful and got on well with most of her clients. She was in her thirties, round-faced and friendly. But she lacked diplomatic skills, tending to dig in her heels when subtlety would have been better. The firm's partners felt that, although she was intelligent and popular, she lacked the flexibility necessary for promotion. Also, she was not ambitious. So she was not on a fast track to partnership.

She tried to keep her tone positive.

"I'm willing to allow ten percent of the expense. That's three million rand which is generous, quite honestly. I am afraid you will have to pay tax on the rest."

"That's not acceptable."

"It's my last word."

Bosu stood up.

"We'll see. There is something else. It involves the casino. I want you to come and have lunch there tomorrow."

The invitation surprised Lucy – it meant flying or driving to Johannesburg – but it was an order, not an enquiry, so she accepted. Joburg Casino, too, was owned by the Bosus and they paid their accounting bills promptly.

~

They were at the casino the next day. It was huge. Outside, life-sized gold statues of lions leaped at visitors through swirling fountains. Lucy felt intimidated even before going inside.

"Come," said Bosu. He led them to the gaming floor.

"What about lunch?" asked Lucy.

"In a minute," said Bosu. "Do you like to gamble?"

"Not really."

They were at a roulette table.

"Give it a try."

"I don't care to. I'm an accountant, I know the odds."

"Just a few rand."

Lucy shook her head.

Impatient, Bosu produced 150 rand in notes, about ten dollars, and handed it to the dealer who slid some chips across to him.

"Put it on," said Bosu. "Place a bet."

"If you insist. Where?"

"Anywhere. What's your favourite number?"

Lucy shrugged and put all the chips on seventeen.

Bosu nodded at the dealer, a bald African in maroon tuxedo and bow tie. The man spun the wheel.

They watched as the little ball clattered round the spinning roulette wheel and came to rest on seventeen.

"Congratulations," said Bosu. "You just won five thousand rand."

The dealer pushed a pile of chips across the table. Lucy put out a hand to remove them.

"Wait," said Bosu. "Leave it on seventeen."

"You must be kidding," said Lucy. "That's a lot of money."

"I have a feeling," said Bosu. He made a signal to the dealer who spun the wheel before Lucy could stop him. Seventeen came up again.

"You're a lucky girl," said Bosu drily. "That makes your winnings nearly two hundred thousand rand."

Lucy was stunned. "What shall I do? Should I leave it on again?"

"I don't think so." Bosu nodded at the dealer who pushed the chips across. Bosu reached in front of Lucy and remove them from the table. "Let's go and cash these in."

The two walked to the cashier's grille and the clerk counted out a thick pile of South African bank notes worth ten thousand dollars and slid it across the counter to Lucy. Still looking startled, she folded it in half and put it away in her purse. Security cameras above the ceiling captured the whole episode.

Bosu patted Lucy on the shoulder.

"Now we can have lunch."

L ater, Dinesh Bosu phoned his middle brother, Haresh, the 'hard man' of the family.

"There's a problem with the audit."

"How come?"

"It's the company picnic. The woman Gray won't allow it as a tax deduction."

"I thought you fixed that. Didn't you slip her twelve grand at the casino?"

"It didn't work."

"Why not?"

"I went to great trouble to make sure she won at roulette."

"Did you use Table Three?"

"Of course. It was impossible for her to lose." Dinesh sounded nervous. He was scared of his brother, always had been. Even as teenagers, Haresh, a couple of years bigger and stronger, thought nothing of wrestling or punching his younger sibling. But it was not just physi-

cal. Haresh was volatile – one minute charming, the next
bullying and contemptuous with no apparent reason for
the change. As an adult, he could still baffle friend and
foe alike by lashing out in ways that were reckless and
cruel.

"So?"

"She thinks she won the money fair and square!"

"Unbelievable," Haresh barked. Dinesh could picture
his scowl, see the thin white scar that curved from the
corner of his mouth all the way to the bottom of his right
ear tightening as he frowned.

"I questioned her decision again after lunch. She
turned me down flat."

"Looks like Plan B, then?"

"Yes."

~

Lucy worked late the next day, finishing at 9 pm. She was
the last person to leave the Bosu building.

She had no idea that she was being watched from the
darkness on the far side of the car park as she got into
her small truck, or "bakkie", for the long drive to Johannesburg. She did a lot of driving, a price she was willing
to pay to live in the metropolis rather than in Biko City,
her place of work, which had much less to offer in the
way of culture or amusement.

Her route home took her through Hillbrow to her flat
in adjoining Berea. Both districts, once fashionable, had
declined since the end of apartheid and were now close

to being slums, noted for crime and poverty. Many of the buildings were spray painted with graffiti although a few, including Ponte City, the huge circular complex where she lived, were in better shape.

The cylindrical Ponte City tower stood fifty-four grey stories high, the tallest residential building in Africa. A red sign wrapped around the top three floors advertised the telephone company Vodacom. The soaring building, built in 1975, once symbolised hopes for a prosperous Johannesburg but the timing had been poor – the economy stalled and the area went downhill. Gangs infiltrated many of the units and the interior courtyard was piled several stories high with garbage.

Today the area was still bad, but Ponte City was starting on its way back up, becoming popular with young professionals thanks to low rents and improved security.

Because Lucy lived where she did, she often had to drive through Hillbrow after dark. It was not a pleasant experience, in fact she sometimes wondered whether she had been wise to move to Ponte City, but she believed strongly in integration and had done so to make a point. The streets were crowded and dirty. Drunks and addicts strolled in the street, darting in front of moving vehicles. Cars parked end to end on both sides of the road, making the way narrow so that traffic moved slowly. Stop signs and yellow lines were treated as suggestions only – sometimes drivers stopped at 'Yield' signs and sometimes they didn't. Cars swerved out of their lane to overtake by the narrowest of margins, threatening to scratch Lucy's paintwork.

Congestion was bad tonight with traffic moving at a crawl. To be safe, she pressed the button on the dash that locked the doors. It made her feel more secure.

She approached a traffic light or 'robot' as stoplights were known in South Africa, a few blocks short of the tower. A dirty grey truck swooped in front of her as she did so, braking at the light. She was glad she had locked her doors.

So the blow from a tyre iron that shattered the driver's window into a thousand pieces was a total shock. Shards of glass rained in, grazing her cheek. A figure in a hoodie leaned in through the shattered pane, reached across to the ignition and pulled out the key.

Lucy flinched in alarm. A second figure leaped from the truck and pulled open the bakkie's other door.

Lucy was sandwiched between the two intruders. One punched her on the chin, a short blow that knocked her senseless. The other replaced the key in the ignition.

The robot turned green. The truck drew smoothly away, followed by the bakkie, and both vehicles vanished into the night.

There were no police around to witness the incident. In the passing crowd several people noticed what happened, but no one was public spirited – or foolhardy – enough to do anything about what they saw.

4

She awoke in the back seat of the speeding truck.

The man beside her was large and solid, smelling of sweat.

Lucy was gentle by nature but she was no coward. "What the hell is this about?" she demanded.

"Never you mind," said her neighbour. The accent was South African and somewhat guttural, rolling his r's, an Afrikaner she thought.

"If it's money you want, you picked the wrong person." It was true, she did not carry much cash, less than fifty dollars. The thought of the money she had won the day before flashed through her mind. She had taken it straight to the bank and paid it in, getting a curious look from the teller. "I got lucky at the casino," she had told him.

"It's not about that," said the man. "Shut up and keep quiet."

"What's your name?" asked Lucy.

"Abel."

"Well, Abel, you had better stop right now and let me out."

"Go play marbles, young lady," he said curtly.

She peered out of the vehicle, her head aching, trying to identify her surroundings. It was dark and at first she could see no landmarks. But a few minutes later she saw an illuminated sign on large, imposing gates that read 'Mediclinic Sandton.' It flashed by and vanished in the dark but she knew immediately that they were in the Bryanston/Sandton area about twelve miles north of Johannesburg. She was familiar with the place, a middle class suburb. It was reassuring not to be in a rougher area, she told herself, then realised how illogical that was – she had just been kidnapped for goodness sake.

After five minutes they turned into a gravel drive. They approached the red and white striped bar of a security gate. There was a kiosk with a uniformed guard and for a moment she thought about shouting for help, but the guard clearly knew the driver because he raised the barrier and waved them through. They drove on past laurel bushes and an expanse of closely mown lawn and stopped in front of a large white house.

She was hustled roughly up shallow stone steps between classical pillars to a double front door. The place looked like a prosperous family's country home, or an exclusive private club in Cape Town. She thought drily that she was cleaner and more in tune with the surroundings than was her sweat-stained captor.

The hallway was decorated in good taste – sofas, silk-shaded lamps on brass stands, a mahogany grandfather clock. The clock struck ten with a deep tone as they stood there. As the notes died away, a door opened and a man appeared. He smiled at Lucy.

"Good evening madam." He was large, probably six foot four and broad shouldered. He looked Indian, in a formal Nehru jacket buttoned to the neck, and was smoking a cigar. He had dark eyes and fierce black eyebrows. Something about the nose and features struck a chord with Lucy. They resembled a more imposing version of Dinesh Bosu.

5

She blinked. "You must be Dinesh's brother, Shiv."

He laughed. "I am flattered to be taken for the head of the family but no, I am not Shiv. I am Haresh Bosu. Dinesh may have mentioned me. I am the *other* brother, you might say."

So this was the tough guy, the enforcer. The one that all the stories were about. "What do you want?" Lucy tried to keep the nervousness out of her voice.

"I am sorry we had to get your attention in this way, but I need to talk to you," said Bosu.

"So, talk." She looked around for a seat and chose a sofa that looked comfortable. She sat down, so that Haresh was forced to sit in an adjoining armchair. She was slowly pulling herself together. These people are very odd, just keep calm, she told herself. Trying to look nonchalant she found a handkerchief and wiped the sweat from her face. Its edge brushed the bruise on her chin and she winced.

Bosu smiled. In better light, the white scar on his cheek was visible. It ran all the way from the right hand corner of his mouth, up across the cheek and ended near the bottom of his right ear. It was thin and straight, as if someone had taken a sharp knife and sliced expertly, but as though a skilled surgeon had then repaired it.

"We need to have a meeting of minds, an understanding about how our family does business."

Lucy frowned. "What sort of understanding? I am an auditor. I have responsibilities. If you take exception to something, then as owners you are welcome to express your views but in a civil way, not through this absurd pantomime!"

Bosu's smile became fixed, but he controlled himself. "Take the matter of the company picnic. It is a business expense and a deduction for tax purposes. That is clear for anyone to see."

She shook her head but said nothing. Bosu went on. "I've spoken to Wickus Van Biljon, the partner in charge and your boss, and he agrees with me."

Lucy did not have a high opinion of Van Biljon even though she reported to him. She considered him provincial and second rate. She herself had graduated near the top of her year at Wits – Witwatersrand University – and had trained with a respected firm of accountants in Pretoria.

"Are you challenging my professional judgement?"

He ignored the question. "There is another matter – the value of the houses being built for the international consortium."

"What about them? I haven't seen them yet."

"You can save yourself the trouble. We've talked to Van Biljon about that too. He is happy with their valuation, so you can accept his opinion."

"If you already have his agreement, why are you bothering me with these matters?"

Bosu frowned. "We know Van Biljon will sign a clean report. But the investors have been showing concern. They may ask questions. We don't want the file to show any signs of dissent. It would be embarrassing."

"Is that so?" Now that Lucy understood what Bosu was concerned about, she felt almost in control. She began to relax.

"Yes," said Bosu. "So, can we have your word on that?"

She pretended to consider the question, but in fact she was perfectly sure of her reply. She shook her head.

"No, I'm sorry. I can't control what Van Biljon may say or do, but if I am not satisfied with some aspect of the audit, my notes will reflect that. It's a matter of principle."

Bosu sighed. "Principle!" He stood up and gave her a look that was partly pitying and partly amused. "You've heard of the expression, 'terminal honesty?'"

"What if I have?"

"That's what you are showing."

"You're being rude."

He shrugged. "We can discuss it in the morning."

"What is there to discuss?"

He ignored the question. "Meanwhile, we shall make

you comfortable upstairs. There is no telephone, but you can watch television if you wish. I bid you good night."

He turned and left the room. The hulking Abel grabbed Lucy by the arm and propelled her roughly upstairs.

"This is your room." Abel indicated a chair outside the door. "I shall be outside."

The room was clean, with a large double bed and its own bathroom. Later, some food arrived – a bowl of spaghetti with meat sauce, and some ice cream. Plain but wholesome. She was surprisingly hungry. She cleaned her plate and put the tray outside the door, nodding at Abel, then settled down for the night.

Or pretended to.

She looked around the room, wondering if there was something she could use as a weapon. Nothing suggested itself. There was a wooden upright chair by the dressing table and she considered breaking a leg off it, but it looked too strong. The chair itself would have to do.

She was still in her work clothes from the office, dark grey skirt and a white blouse that by now was scuffed and grubby. She took off her shoes and skirt. She washed her face, removing the thin gold chain and locket that she always wore. She put them in a small closet above the washbasin in the bathroom for safe keeping. Then she climbed into bed and switched off the light.

She waited half an hour, then got out of bed, dressed quietly and put on her shoes. She arranged a bolster sideways under the covers in a makeshift simulation of a sleeping body, not too convincing but it would have to do. Then she tiptoed over to the door and took up a position behind it with the chair raised above her head. She called out, "Abel!"

No reply. She shouted again, "Abel!"

A minute later the door opened. Abel stood in the doorway, looking toward the darkened bed. He had a pistol in his hand. With all her strength, Lucy brought the chair down on his head. One blow was enough. His body collapsed on the carpet. Lucy grabbed the pistol and stuffed it in the waistband of her skirt before tiptoeing downstairs. As she crept through the hallway the grandfather clock chimed. It was one-thirty in the morning.

In seconds she was out of the door.

She felt the cool night air on her face. She allowed herself a brief feeling of triumph at being free but then focused her mind on the problem ahead. She must hurry – Abel would recover soon.

She set about finding her way out of the estate by retracing her steps along the driveway to the gate. She merged close to the bushes as she approached the white painted kiosk. There was no light in the cabin and no guard, and she slipped out into the open road.

So here she was, a lone pedestrian in the middle of the night. In some parts of Johannesburg that would be a risky situation but here in Bryanston she felt moderately safe.

The problem was that she had no idea in which direction to go. A bright half moon had risen but she had no clue what its location would tell her, being a dunce when it came to navigation.

She flipped a mental coin and set out towards where a localised brightening in the sky suggested that there might be buildings around the corner.

A hundred yards on, she felt a surge of optimism. The source of the light was a 24 hour service station in the green and yellow colours of BP. That meant people, perhaps an Uber cab, and a return to her comfortable apartment.

She almost made it. She was only fifty yards short of the gleaming oasis when the blow landed from behind. The force was so great that she never had time to wonder what hit her before blackness engulfed her senses.

Y ou're still in London? Why haven't you left?"
It was my abrasive boss Carlton, phoning from Tortola. A simple question but with an edge as usual.

"I'm leaving tonight, for Pete's sake. Your creepy friend Coward only got here today." I try to be polite to Carlton but it's difficult.

He grunted disapprovingly.

For those who don't know, my boss Carlton Tisch is a rich but annoying investment banker. He is small physically, but a heavyweight financially as a result of founding the largest receivables financing company on the east coast of the United States. You don't need to know what receivables financing is; just be aware that it is a very profitable line of business.

He is the son of poor Russian immigrants and in many ways embodies the American dream. His parents ran a small deli on Manhattan's Lower East Side, but the young Carlton was not satisfied with cooking up blintzes and knishes and got a menial job at Goldman Sachs, sorting mail. He went on to become a billionaire at thirty. Gifted painter, adequate sailor, now in his sixties, he lives on Tortola and does a couple of deals a year with at least eight zeros on the end, making it all look easy.

He finds me useful because I am single, unattached and willing to travel while he enjoys the company of his nubile third wife on the sunny terrace of his cliff-top villa at the far western end of Tortola. Despite my expensive education, which is vastly superior to his, I sometimes feel like the pilot fish that accompanies the shark. What me, jealous?

"I've been lining things up for you in South Africa," he said.

"How very kind." In my mind I could see the skinny, suntanned financier in shorts and Yankees baseball cap, relaxing in the sunshine, scowling as usual.

"Here's your cover story: you are an accountant with LevyTeagardenHooper – LTH as they are known – auditors of the Bosu companies. Shiv Bosu, the senior Bosu brother, is the man we entrusted our money to. There are two younger brothers, Haresh and Dinesh. Dinesh, also known as Danny, is the manager of Bosu Construction who are building the affordable housing. Go and see him."

"What about Shiv and Haresh?"

"Shiv is the real boss, a very smooth operator. Haresh is the enforcer, the tough guy. He's slightly crazy."

"Paul Coward said that about Haresh. Also that he had a glass eye and a scar. I wasn't sure if he was joking."

"He wasn't joking. The man must have been in a fight somewhere."

"Have you met him?"

"Briefly, just a few words when we signed the contract. They say he has a violent streak."

"Not a good thing, commercially."

Carlton laughed. "You might be surprised. There's a definite place for the wild card in business, it can sometimes give you a winning hand. Anyway, ignore the older brothers for now. Concentrate on Dinesh."

"Okay."

"Report to him when you get to Biko City, the capital of Protea. You are an extra hand, sent to help because the audit is behind schedule. I've fixed it with LTH in New York."

"What's he like?"

"Dinesh? Skinny little tyke. He's the least evil of the three brothers but I don't trust any of them."

"Sounds like we'll all be bosom pals."

"Before you meet Dinesh, call in at the auditors' office in Biko City. The partner in charge is an Afrikaner, Van Biljon. Don't trust him either."

"Is that an order or an opinion?"

He ignored me.

"One more thing. There's a girl you should meet."

"That sounds better."

"Her name is Rebekka Moran. She's with the Chicago

Consulting Group. There's some funny business going on between her firm and another Bosu subsidiary."

"What sort of funny business?"

"I don't know. Coward mentioned it. You'll have to find out for yourself."

And that was all the preparation I got for my in-depth investigation into major fraud in South Africa.

8

I stretched uncomfortably in my airplane seat. The flight from London to Johannesburg takes eleven hours. The Boeing 787 Dreamliner left Heathrow at 7 pm and would touch down at Johannesburg's Oliver Tambo airport just after breakfast, which was being served by Jasmine, a young Indian stewardess with a delightful South African accent.

I did some research, meaning that we chatted.

"Tell me what life is like now for the non-African population in South Africa?"

She frowned. "It's okay I suppose, but uncertain. When Nelson Mandela was released from Robben Island in 1982 – he remained in other prisons until 1990 – whites were twenty percent of the population. Today they are only ten percent."

"Why?"

"Concerns about the political future. Inefficient government. Corruption, too – that's getting scary."

"Corruption where?"

"In government. There was always petty corruption, but nowadays it's worse. In the old days, if you wanted to jump the queue for a new phone, you left a case of scotch with the man at the telephone company. But the problems now are bigger. They go all the way to the top."

"Give me an example."

"An Indian family is accused of bribing the recent ex-President so thoroughly that the state electrical utility cancelled its contract to buy coal and made a new deal with a company owned by the Indians."

"Is that truth or rumour?"

"I don't know. But the President just quit under pressure."

"That's shocking."

Jasmine nodded sadly, her smooth face troubled. "State capture, that's what they call it. As an Indian I feel deeply pained by the situation, it has given us such a bad name. In the hundred years from Gandhi to multiparty democracy, Indians were seen as selfless givers, but now with one fell swoop we are seen as corrupt thugs by the Africans."

"I understand your discomfort."

She nodded. "I am from Durban, where Gandhi first settled. He set up the oldest political party in South Africa and these developments would cause him only shame."

"Do you think things will improve under the new President?"

She shrugged. "He is making all the right noises. We'll have to see."

9

S hortly after dawn, we landed at Oliver Tambo Airport. I just had time to stop at the Vodacom kiosk to buy something called a "Tourist Sim Card" for my mobile phone. The girl installed it for me, using a scarlet fingernail to slide it in. Then I sprinted through the terminal to the gate for the next leg of my journey.

The forty seat Brazilian Embraer jet was half full. There was a 'Daily Sun' newspaper on the next seat, left behind by a previous passenger. The lead story was about the Indian brothers Jasmine had mentioned. They were accused of bribing the former president and then using their influence to secure lucrative contracts with a government agency.

It was intriguing stuff, whether true or false, but I hardly had time to scan the article before we were fastening our seat belts for landing.

◇

After Gauteng, which until 1994 was known as Transvaal, Protea is the second wealthiest province in South Africa thanks to gold and coal, but its rural areas are dirt poor. It is east of Gauteng and west of Mpumalanga. The main languages are Tswana and Zulu, but in the capital, Biko City, English and Afrikaans are spoken.

My destination was Bosu Construction on the edge of town, but first I had to visit LTH, the company's auditors.

My taxi passed mining company offices, banks, accountants and lawyers, the kind of professional infrastructure that goes along with being at the centre of a mining area. The headquarters of the *Protea Times* was also there. A block farther on was the office of LTH, LevyTeagardenHooper, one of the world's largest firms of accountants.

It was not a huge office. LTH had grown big by absorbing smaller independent firms, and I guessed this had been one of them. I paid the cab driver, straightened my tie and went inside.

10

T he blonde at the front desk was attractive but severe, she looked used to putting people in their place. A poor first impression. Was it an omen?

"Wickus Van Biljon, please."

"And you are?"

"Oliver Steele."

"Is he expecting you?"

"Probably."

"What's that supposed to mean?"

I smiled. "Just call him."

She did, and what she heard did not seem to make her any happier. "You can go on in." Another friend not made. Oh well.

Van Biljon's office was dark and obsessively neat, and so was he. Pale face, no smile, greasy black hair. A small Hitler moustache that made him look even worse –

hadn't anyone told him? He did not get up from his chair when I walked in.

He gave me a weak handshake.

I knew I wouldn't like him. It never takes me long to decide and no exception here.

11

"**I** have no idea why New York sent you," he said. He had a strong Afrikaans accent that I had to strain to understand.

I smiled. "Nice to see you too."

He sighed. "But it so happens we need help at Bosu Construction. My audit manager, Lucy Gray, didn't show up for work today. She isn't answering her phone and the audit is supposed to be finished by Friday, so your timing is actually not too bad."

"Okay," I said cheerfully.

"Ach, you had better get on over there." He eyed me, doubt on his face. "They say you were a partner at a firm in London."

I nodded, trying to display my partner face. That phase of my life is something I would rather forget.

"What happened?" he asked.

"The firm dissolved." It was my stock response. Actually, the senior partner tricked me into signing a fraudulent balance sheet. He went to prison. I very nearly went down with him but the judge took pity on me, thanks to my youth and inexperience. But I chose to accept full responsibility for the million pound loss incurred by the client. That's why I am bankrupt.

"Where did you go next?"

"I started my own firm," I said glibly. I've uttered the evasion so often I'm fluent with it. The truth is that I ran away to Florida and have been bumming work from Carlton Tisch ever since.

"I suppose you'll do," he said. "I would finish the audit myself but I'm very busy, so the ball is in your court."

"I have a question," I said.

He looked at his watch. "Yes?"

"I've been hearing stories about the Bosu brothers. Can you tell me something about them?"

"What do you want to know?"

"For starters, are there any transactions between Bosu Construction and the Bosus as individuals that might violate their contract with the joint venture?"

The Hitler moustache twitched. "Absolutely not."

"I've heard that the middle brother, Haresh, does some quite unconventional things. So I wondered."

"Haresh is a fine gentleman and a respected client of LTH."

"How did he get the scar on his face?"

He frowned. "That's none of your business. It is also impertinent. Go over there and meet your colleagues. Here's the file."

I left with that frosty non-endorsement ringing in my ears. Onwards to Bosu Construction and no doubt a barrel-load of fun.

I rented a car from Hertz and headed for Bosu's premises. As I approached, it became clear that I was in a shabby area on the edge of town. Was that to save on rent? Nothing wrong with that. The company should be spending money on its core purpose, not on smart offices.

In the lobby, I asked where the auditors were working.

"In the conference room. Second door on the left." The receptionist was pretty, she looked Indian.

I set off down the corridor. I was intercepted by a thin faced man in a dark suit.

"Oliver Steele?"

"That's me."

"I'm Dinesh Bosu. Wickus Van Biljon at LTH said you were coming."

He pumped my hand and smiled, or tried to. Smiling didn't seem to come easily.

"So you're the new audit manager?"

"Temporarily. I'm substituting for Lucy Gray who is sick."

"Of course, of course. His eyes swivelled away from mine. He rubbed his hands together and shifted from foot to foot. "Well, you'll find things pretty straight-forward."

It's been a few years since I audited a company, but I remember a couple of things very well: managers mistrust auditors and things are always 'pretty straight-forward.'

I smiled. "Let's hope so."

He seemed to be trying to analyse my reply. Only three words for goodness sake, what was there to analyse?

"Well, if you have any issues, we can sort them out."

"Of course."

He thought about that, looking at the floor.

"Better get on," I said brightly. I moved to pass him in the narrow corridor. He stepped reluctantly aside.

In the conference room I introduced myself to the other two auditors, Jerrie Naudé and Victor Mbutu. Both were qualified accountants in their twenties. Jerrie was an Afrikaner, short and with a pleasant smile, with just a slight accent. Victor, African, was thin-framed in black slacks and blue shirt and looked studious behind his glasses.

"You've certainly come a long way," said Jerrie. "And your timing is excellent, you are in time for the annual *braai*."

"The what?"

"The *braai*. Short for *braaivleis* which means 'roasted meat' in Afrikaans. It's the South African version of a barbecue. LTH has one every year for employees and clients. It's this week."

"I don't know if I'm invited. Van Biljon didn't say anything about it."

"I'm sure you are, but I'll check if you like."

"Thanks. So how's the work going?"

"We're about finished," said Victor.

Jerrie nodded. "We've done all the routine testing. The books look clean."

"Lucy had a few questions," said Victor. "She made a list."

I found it in the file. Two items stood out:

'Verify housing'

And

'The expensive picnic'

I tapped the page. "*Verify housing.* What did she mean?"

"She wanted to go and inspect the homes the company is building," said Victor. "With thirty-seven million U.S. dollars spent it's the biggest item on the balance sheet by far, so clearly it should be verified."

"Makes sense," I said. "Someone should take a look. Where are they located?"

"A couple of hours drive from here."

"May be a dumb question but shouldn't we have done that already? The audit is supposed to be finished this week."

Victor said, "Lucy discussed it with Mr. Bosu last week. He said it was a bad time. A subcontractor does the actual construction and he was out of town."

"The trouble is, he told her the same thing when we first got here," said Jerrie.

I had heard enough. "I'll have a word with Mr. Bosu."

"Good luck," said Victor.

"What's that supposed to mean?"

"He's not very approachable."

"Well he's going to be approached now. Where's his office?"

"Down the hall."

I knocked on Bosu's door. There was no reply. I knocked again and entered.

He was talking on the speaker phone. He shook his head at me, but I just smiled and sat down.

The conversation was about money and I could hear both sides. The other party spoke English with an accent.

"TransOcean will pay three percent."

"Is that the best you can do?" asked Bosu. "I can get four percent here."

"In rands. But then you would have the exchange risk."

Bosu caught my eye. He frowned and switched languages. He ended the conversation, his last words barked rather than spoken.

Indian banknotes are printed in sixteen different languages besides English, so he could be speaking Hindi, Tamil or any of fourteen others. But one thing was obvious – he did not wish me to know what he was saying.

"This conversation is personal," he said. "What do you want?"

"I'd like to look at the homes."

His face froze. "Why?"

"Auditors verify assets. It's what we do."

"Those homes are still under construction. That

means you must value them based on the amount spent. You already know that figure."

Remember to smile. "Of course. It's a formality, what we call best practice."

"Best practice . . . " He rolled the words around his mouth as if they were bitter. The laboured smile again. "Very well. I'll make the arrangements and get back to you."

"Please do. Time is short."

The phone rang a bit later, when I was back with the auditors. Victor handed it to me.

"This is Van Biljon."

My new boss. "Yes?"

"I need you back here."

"But I only just arrived."

"Now, if you please."

I drove back thinking, *this is time wasted.*

It was late afternoon when I reached the LTH office again. This time I walked straight past the blonde and into Van Biljon's room. He looked even darker than before.

"How did you find things?" he asked.

"Pretty far along," I said. "Just a couple of loose ends."

"Leave the real estate alone," he said.

"Meaning?"

"You don't need to go there."

"Really?"

He shook his head. "I went myself a few weeks ago."

"And?"

"Everything's fine. No issues."

"Glad to hear that."

"Yes. So you can value them at their cost in the balance sheet, no problem."

"That's peachy," I said.

He frowned.

"Did Dinesh Bosu just phone you?" I asked.

The temperature, already low, fell several degrees.

He looked at his watch.

"That will be all."

12

I felt I had done enough for one day. There was a Southern Sun motel in town. I checked in, unpacked my bag and then went down to the restaurant where I ate a halfway decent steak. Then I watched the news on CNN and went to bed.

I did not go back to Bosu Construction next morning. Instead, I telephoned Jerrie Naudé.

"What's the name of the head guy at the contractors, the people who build the houses?"

"Danie Basson. Do you want me to call him?"

"No, that's okay. Give me his phone number."

"I'll text it to you. Do you want the address, as well? It's near Kloofdorp."

"Yes, please."

Jerrie said, "I checked with Van Biljon, incidentally – you are invited to the *braai*."

"That's good. Last time we spoke he didn't seem too friendly."

"He's often like that. You shouldn't think anything of it."

"Okay." But I wasn't sure I agreed.

"The *braai* will be fun. You'll get introduced to *boerewors* and *mealie pap*."

"Translation?"

He laughed. "*Boerewors* is a special South African sausage. *Mealie pap* is a sort of porridge made of coarsely ground maize."

"Sounds like grits."

"Maybe."

"Is there any news of Lucy Gray?" I asked.

"No. It's worrying."

"When was she last seen?"

"She was still at the office when Victor and I left around six-thirty, two nights ago."

"Nothing since then?"

"Not a word."

"What about her car?"

"It had gone from the car park, so she left the premises."

"Did she arrive home?"

"Not according to the police. They went in and checked her flat in Ponte City."

"Ponte City? I thought she lived in Johannesburg."

"Ponte City is in Joburg. It's a huge residential tower with a dubious past – it was once a very smart address but after democracy and white flight from central Joburg it fell on hard times."

"Odd place for a professional woman to live. Do you think she may have been mugged in that building?"

"Unlikely," said Jerrie. "It's very strictly controlled nowadays and much safer, with 24-hour security gates, fingerprint sensors, the whole nine yards. Besides, her truck is missing. So whatever happened to her must have happened on her way home."

"Where do you think she is now?" I asked.

"Who knows?"

"Well," I said, "one problem at a time. By the way . . ."

"Yes?"

"If Dinesh Bosu asks where I am, you don't know. I'm out of the office on personal business. I may come in towards the end of the day."

"Got it."

~

The farther away I got from Biko City, the more wide-open and lonely the landscape became. The city centre gave way first to suburbs and then to tawny veldt with short grass the colour of dirty sand. Here and there an umbrella thorn or baobab tree jutted up, and occasionally a clump of sugarbush dotted with protea, the pink national flower of South Africa that gave the province its name.

I came at last to a faded wooden sign saying Kloofdorp. I would have missed it if I hadn't keyed the address into the car's sat-nav, because there was almost nothing there.

I don't know what I had expected – perhaps a street of dwellings with a corner store or gas station. Instead, there was just a row of three long single-storey buildings, unfinished, made of concrete block. Each had a blue tarpaulin stretched over the roof's rafters to keep out the weather. The doors were unpainted. The small windows contained plywood, not glass.

Each building contained eight dwellings a side. From the way the windows were arranged, one or two bedrooms at the most. They reminded me of the grim housing known as 'back-to-backs' thrown up in the north of England during the Industrial Revolution.

I drove round behind. Sure enough, they were in back-to-back format, so each building accommodated sixteen units.

A few yards from the back of each building stood a row of white privy cubicles of the temporary kind. But in this case they were bolted to a concrete foundation, suggesting they were intended as crude permanent toilets.

Back-to-back houses in Britain were inherently cramped and poorly ventilated and most of them were demolished by the end of the 19th Century. But here in Protea, apparently, history was repeating itself and not in a good way.

I wondered how to value the development. I had not researched South African housing but the area was remote, so the land probably represented little cost. I did some quick sums. There were forty-eight dwelling units. Even at twenty thousand dollars each, which was gener-

ous, their total value would be less than a million
dollars. Allowing for site clearance and utilities maybe
two million, tops. Yet the asset sat in Bosu's balance sheet
at thirty-seven million dollars. Where was the missing
thirty-five million?

I had seen enough. I pulled out my phone and called
the number Jerrie had given me.

"Basson." A gruff voice.

"Mr. Basson, this is Oliver Steele, the auditor of Bosu
Construction. I am in the area, can I come round and see
you?"

"Sure." He sounded brusque but encouraging, not
like a man with a bad conscience.

A few minutes later I was sitting in his air-conditioned office four miles away in tiny Kloofdorp, drinking
his coffee.

He raised bushy eyebrows and smiled, inviting me to
speak. He was solidly built and wore a checked shirt and
dark slacks, his waistline fighting a losing battle with a
generous belly. A red face indicated either high blood
pressure or too much time in the sun. Dark, slicked-back
hair surmounted brown eyes, the sockets wrinkled at the
corners. He looked about fifty.

"I'll come straight to the point," I said. "I am here to
look at the development and I was shocked at how cheap
those homes are."

Basson nodded. "It's a fair comment." He paused.
"From your accent you're new to South Africa?"

"Yes."

"Well you're right, the housing is basic. But it's what

the customer ordered. And it beats what these rural blacks are used to." He pronounced it *'blecks.'* In Britain or the United States his remark would have smacked of racism. Was the thinking different here where whites were in the minority?

He gave me a glance. "Did I shock you?"

He obviously went in for plain speaking, so gloves off. I was here to discuss money, not race relations.

"I'm trying to understand how Bosu Construction spent thirty-seven million dollars here, all of it paid to you?"

He shrugged. "I certainly received that money, but I didn't keep it."

"How so?"

"Read the contract. I agreed a price with Bosu and the job is coming in right on the button. But my biggest payments by a mile are the fees to the architect that Bosu makes me use."

'When all else fails, read the contract!' It was a maxim I fully endorsed but in this case I hadn't done so. I felt foolish.

"Let me be sure I understand. You don't keep the money you get from Bosu?"

"I keep some of it. But I also have to pay the architect."

"No offense, but can you prove that?"

"Sure I can. You want to talk in dollars? I've made transfers adding up to thirty-five million dollars in the past year."

"Just for designing those plain buildings?"

"Correct. And it's front loaded, I had to pay it first."

"Really?"

"Sure. It's all in my bank statements, with transfers to the account of Essential Architects Inc. at TransOcean Bank in Dubai."

He pulled a green folder from a drawer in his metal desk. It took him a minute to find the page but then he turned the file round so that I could read it.

"You can look if you don't believe me."

There were half a dozen transfers of about six million dollars each, all paid to an architectural firm in Dubai.

"I said I trusted you," I said.

He smiled drily. "Trust but verify, eh?"

I got up to leave. "Thanks for your help. You've been very forthcoming."

"Yes, I have," he said. "And you're welcome. But since you clearly want to get to the bottom of things, let me tell you about something else."

Previously relaxed, he suddenly sounded tense.

"I'm guessing you've not heard of PBF, the Protea Business Forum?"

"You guess right."

"It's ostensibly a labour organization. Not a trade union exactly, but a sort of semi-military organization that defends the rights of African workers."

"The motive sounds righteous enough."

"The *motive* is. But unfortunately, PBF can be bought, like so much in this damn country nowadays."

"Not so good."

"And Bosu bought their services."

"In connection with this housing?"

"Sure."

"What does that mean? How does it affect your business here?"

"It means I have to get PFB approval for the workers I employ. All workers must be local residents."

"That does not sound unreasonable."

"It's not. I'd have done it anyway."

"Then what's the problem?"

He laughed bitterly. "I just don't like being dictated to by an armed gang."

"Armed?"

"I was visited by a so-called Forum rep, a big, thick-necked guy with a Ruger automatic on his hip. He said he just wanted to underline the ground rules."

"Enforcement was implied?"

He nodded. "To give you an idea, in another part of the province an industrial project ground to a halt when a PBF gang invaded the site and burned the buildings to the ground. There have been other cases where employees had guns pointed at them, were slapped around and had to flee through the bush."

"So you agreed with everything he said?"

Basson nodded. "You don't mess around with the PFB. Some call them the construction Mafia."

He sighed. "On the other hand, I must admit Bosu is a good payer. Some customers you have to chase for money, but not Bosu. I do what they ask. I do it on time.

The price is generous and they come through on the nail."

Sure, I thought. *With all the money they are making they can afford to keep you happy.*

He shrugged philosophically. "Times have changed in South Africa. Construction has always been a tough business but I honestly think that, since democracy," he paused and laughed shortly, "that's what they call it, the period since the first free elections in 1994. Anyway, since democracy, things have been getting worse, not better. Nowadays, you do business with all sorts of people."

"Maybe it's just a transitional period," I said, trying to sound sympathetic. "Political teething trouble."

He laughed bleakly. "Teething trouble? It's been a quarter of a century already."

As I left he was gazing out of the window. He might have been having doubts of some kind, it was hard to tell.

Where had I heard of TransOcean Bank?

13

Back at the Southern Sun I headed for the bar. Auditing is thirsty work.

"What's the best local beer?" I asked the bartender.

He pointed to a coaster on the polished wood counter.

It read *Black Label sê die Bybel.*

"Translation, please."

"It means *The Bible says one should drink Black Label.*"

The first pint went down smoothly, and I ordered another.

"Good?" he asked.

"Outstanding."

At a table nearby, half a dozen beefy young men in navy blazers were speaking Afrikaans. They had short hair, pink complexions and thick necks. Most of them looked in their twenties. An older man was doing most of the talking. His deep, guttural phrases had an almost musical lilt. He seemed to be delivering some kind of lecture.

I couldn't understand anything at first but then the odd English phrase – *touchdown, offside* – gave the game away. He was a rugby coach motivating his players. It was just about sports, but his intensity was arresting and I was oddly moved. I felt like an eavesdropper peeping through a window into the Afrikaners' soul. Jasmine had mentioned on the plane that the percentage of whites in South Africa had halved in recent years, but clearly no-one should underestimate the massive permanence of people like these in the national fabric.

I went upstairs to my room and phoned Carlton. With the clock difference, it was 12 noon which is cock-tail time on Tortola.

I could hear the clink of glasses. "What?" he barked.

"Am I interrupting anything?"

"Yes. Joe Chapman is here. We're organising the Tortola Open Squash Tournament, which is next month." Joe was the island squash champion, ranked in the world's top hundred.

"Oh, excuse me."

"Never mind," he said more graciously. "What have you learned?"

"Dinesh Bosu is seriously dishonest."

"Can you be more specific?"

"You know those houses on Bosu's balance sheet, the ones listed at thirty-seven million?"

"Well?"

"I went and looked at them. What I saw is very odd."

"Odd how?"

"The buildings are unfinished. They are cheap and nasty. But most important, thirty-five of the thirty-seven million dollars spent went to the architects. It was funnelled through a subcontractor, so the fact will not be visible in Bosu's published accounts."

From the silence on the line, I could tell I had his attention.

"The aforesaid architects bank with TransOcean Bank in Dubai. And earlier today I overheard Dinesh Bosu talking to TransOcean about how much interest they would pay on deposits. You don't have to be a genius to connect the dollar signs."

"Who are TransOcean Bank?"

"I don't know, but they have an office in Dubai."

"I'll check with Paul Coward, he does a bit of business there."

"Here's another thing: it's not just Bosu that is the problem. I'm starting to wonder about the auditors. The managing partner Van Biljon makes me nervous. He ordered me not to inspect the houses on the company's balance sheet. Said he had checked them out himself. I went anyway, under my own steam."

I heard the splash of someone diving in the pool. "Are you sure I'm not interrupting anything?"

"Mimi and Kathy are having a swim. But you're way off base about LevyTeagardenHooper. They are the third biggest accounting firm in the world. For them to be in league with the Bosus is unthinkable."

Carlton is impressed by size, something to do with

coming up from nowhere. Odd, considering how shrewd he is generally.

"If you say so," I said. But I still had my doubts about Van Biljon.

Time to change the subject.

"What else do you know about the Bosus?" I asked.

"Shiv and his brothers wormed their way into the inner circle of Protea's politicians and then used their influence to win sweetheart contracts for their businesses. We did not hear about all this until after we had got into business with them. I guess we should have done our due diligence more thoroughly, but we were just not expecting anything like that. Critics call it State capture."

"Sounds thoroughly corrupt."

"Or thoroughly smart," he said. "Isn't that how most business is done?"

I know Carlton so I expect flip remarks from him, but he was quite serious.

"Well the Bosus may have gone a step too far," I said. "I've been reading the local newspapers. This fellow Maputo, Protea's Minister of Finance, recently spent over a hundred thousand dollars on his home, adding a tennis court and a bowling alley. People are asking where he got the money. It's been suggested it came from the Bosus in exchange for appointing them coal suppliers to Pelec, Protea's electrical utility."

"So?" asked Carlton.

"So you have to wonder if the money flowed in a

circle: from Pelec to the Bosus for coal and then – some of it – from the Bosus back to the Minister?"

"Really?" Carlton was starting to sound bored. He has a short attention span for ideas not his own.

"Did you meet Rebekka Moran yet?" he asked.

"No, but I'm off to Johannesburg shortly. I'll check in with her then."

"Her project for Chicago Consulting involves cleaning up a rigged purchasing system at the province's electricity supplier."

"More crookery? What the heck is going on in South Africa?" I asked.

"That's why you're there – to find out. Keep digging."

I sighed. "Leave it with me. I'll try and figure out who's screwing who."

"Take care," said Carlton. He didn't sound as if he meant it.

" Why? Am I in physical danger?"

"Anything's possible."

"You're so reassuring."

14

"Damn," said Shiv Bosu, head of the Bosu family.

The plump faced Indian was reading the Protea Times in his Biko City office.

The day's headline read:

"Bosu Brothers stealing from government *again*?"

The article described a lawsuit filed by Bosu Electric, one of his companies, against the municipal government of Protea. It was an attempt to compel payment for services rendered.

He tossed the newspaper away with a frown.

His middle brother Haresh was in the room and also his financial director, Basil Heinie. Heinie was visiting. He normally worked in Bosu's office in Dubai where he coordinated the group's financial affairs. He had already seen the article. He glanced at Shiv, trying to read his thoughts.

"The publicity is regrettable," he said cautiously.

Shiv Bosu and Heinie were both in their fifties but in most other ways they were a contrast. Bosu was an Indian from Andhra Pradesh. He looked thoughtful and calm. His sonorous voice lent weight to his words and, besides a fluency in Telugu that betrayed his Dravidian cultural heritage he spoke better English than most Britishers, thanks to an expensive Indian boarding school where the teachers themselves were British. He managed to convey that, for him, business was just an intellectual game and making money a side effect that did not greatly interest him, although in fact nothing could be further from the truth. This manner, and a subtle brain, made him the centre of attention in most business discussions.

Basil Heinie, in contrast, was skinny, thin-cheeked and beak-nosed, with grey hair receding from a domed forehead, anxious-looking and essentially without humour. He was coloured in the sense the term was used in South Africa, meaning that he had some African blood. He had grown up speaking Afrikaans in Cape Flats, a lower middle class district of Cape Town, and although his English was fluent he had a definite accent.

"Things seem to be getting pretty hot for us here," said Shiv. "We need to take stock."

"That's just what I've been telling you," said Heinie. "The technique we use, state capture if you must call it that, has a limited life span. We find politicians who are susceptible – not hard to do. We gain control over them, and then we exploit them for profit. That has worked well here but the end of the cycle may be near."

"It has worked perfectly," interrupted Haresh.

Heinie shrugged. "Until now, yes. But in its wake comes criticism. It's inevitable. It's part of democracy and of having a so-called free press. The next stage is political opposition and the sort of investigations that are going on at Bosu Construction and at Pelec."

"You're too defeatist," barked Haresh.

He was the youngest and largest of the three men. His presence was intimidating, six foot four and broad, running to fat. Thick black eyebrows and moustache. His right eye was made of glass. It seemed not to swivel when the other did, even though it was expensive and made with great precision. He was three years younger than Shiv but larger, with the air of a bully and a loud voice given to aggressive statements. His companions were used to his impatient outbursts which could nevertheless bring reasoned discussion to an abrupt halt.

"These investigators are certainly a problem," said Shiv. "What's your solution?"

"Kill them."

Shiv sighed.

"I mean it," said Haresh. "All of them. The auditor Lucy Gray, the Moran woman and now this accountant Steele who has just arrived from England."

There was silence in the room. Shiv did not take his brother literally, but nobody dismissed the idea out of hand.

15

Heinie broke the silence.

"That's a bit strong."

Haresh rounded on him. "Why?"

"It's unnecessary."

"Unnecessary? When all our income is at risk?"

Heinie shook his head. "Not true. If you looked at the monthly financial statements I send you, you would see that we get as much income from our activities in Zimbabwe, where we have bought the co-operation of several cabinet ministers since Mugabe left office, as we do from Protea."

Haresh shrugged. He never read financial statements.

"What about Guinea," asked Shiv. He was referring to the nation of Guinea-Malia, one of four African countries with the word Guinea in their name. "You've been spending time with the President there. Is he susceptible?"

Heinie shook his head. "There's nothing doing for

now. The President is not corrupt, but he is old and his wits are starting to fail him. I think we can get control of the copper industry in that country. It will be a huge payday, but it will take a while. Perhaps in a year's time..."

"Good," said Shiv. "Are you going to Guinea-Malia now?"

"No, I have to return to Dubai. I have matters to attend to."

"What matters?" Over the years Shiv had come to rely heavily on the South African accountant but he still felt a need to check up on him occasionally.

"Renewing bank deposits on better terms, things like that. My signature is required. Annoying but necessary."

"Well, let's think about all these things," said Shiv. He stood up, indicating that the meeting was over.

Haresh indicated the newspaper. "There's an article by Maputo, too." Maputo was the province's Minister of Finance.

"I read it," said Shiv. He smiled. "He's going on and on about the importance of financial integrity in government."

"Is that amusing?" asked Haresh.

Shiv stared at him. "Not amusing, but interesting. Maputo thinks he can treat the public like fools. He has no idea how vulnerable he is."

"To whom?"

"To the media, mainly. He has been accepting our favours for so long that he has come to regard it as proper, but in the eyes of the public it's illegal. And the press, who consider themselves the conscience of the world, will wring the last drop of drama from his behaviour when the truth comes out, as it will."

"We should dispose of Maputo, too," said Haresh.

Shiv shook his head in annoyance. "You seem to think that's the answer to every problem. It is not, especially with a public figure like Maputo. We must use finesse, not force." He liked the sound of the phrase and repeated it. "Finesse, not force."

Haresh scowled. "If you say so."

"I do. Changing the subject, what's going on at Bosu Construction?"

Haresh shrugged. "The auditor won't accept our tax treatment of the company picnic."

"How much money is involved?"

"Two million dollars."

"That's significant."

Haresh nodded. "We've already taken action."

"What does that mean?"

"The auditor Gray is enjoying an involuntary stay at my house in Bryanston."

There was silence for a minute. Shiv shook his head. "You must be careful."

"I'm always careful."

"Don't harm her. This is not the Mumbai slums where disappearances are commonplace."

Haresh wondered how much to tell his brother about Lucy. He shrugged. "Our brother Dinesh is weak, he should never have got into a stupid argument about tax law. But since he has, we need to send a strong message."

"Strong messages are fine but there are many ways to

send a message. There is no need for violence. We pay LTH several million in fees, that's our trump card. We just need to hint that we are thinking of changing auditors and they will sit up and pay attention."

Haresh shrugged. "I'll speak to Dinesh. We'll take care of it, one way or another."

"Good," said Shiv. "We don't want the company picnic to become a national headline."

"Of course not."

Shiv was still uneasy. He had made Dinesh manager of Bosu Construction because he thought there was no scope for the youngest brother to make mistakes there.

After Haresh left, he went over to the window and stood looking out at the Biko City skyline. He thought for a few minutes then went back to his desk and picked up the telephone.

16

I wasn't sure what to wear for a *braai*. The only person I could think to consult was my fellow auditor Jerrie Naudé, so I phoned him.

"Dress casually, as if you were going to a barbecue in the United States," he said. "Victor and I have been invited with our wives, so we'll see you there."

I dug out a white short-sleeved shirt that was reasonably informal. Not very festive but it would have to do. I travel light. I try and fit everything into a carry-on bag because I hate to check luggage in the hold and then wait for ages staring at the carousel where it is invariably the last to arrive.

The *braai* was at the home of Wickus Van Biljon in the suburbs of Biko City. The invitation was for seven pm. It was getting dark when I arrived but I could see that I was in a wooded district with some big houses. The LTH partner's home was as big as any of them. The accounting business apparently provided Wickus a good living.

Numerous cars, many of them large and expensive, were parked on the gravel driveway and extending into the street and across the road, with more still arriving. I followed the flow of people round the side of the house and all the way back past a tennis court and swimming pool to the edge of the woods.

Small wrought iron tables were scattered around a clearing for guests to sit and eat at. People were clustered around the grill which was near the trees and lit by spotlights attached to the trees at a height of about twelve feet.

They illuminated clusters of people talking and laughing loudly. The grill had apparently been lit for some time and was now mature, its logs glowing orange. There was a delicious smell of burning applewood and occasional sparks flew up when the flames hit an unusually dry patch.

Several dozen men and women clustered around the grill, many holding beer cans – it looked like an even split between Windhoek and Black Label with here and there a Bud Light for a touch of U.S. influence. The people looked a well-fed lot. Colourful checked shirts with jeans and calf-length crocodile boots seemed to be the preferred dress – casual but self-consciously clean. Affluence seemed to be the keynote and I marked them down as clients of LTH rather than employees.

My host, Wickus Van Biljon, was the centre of attention and conversation. He had undergone a transformation since our meeting in his office. The sports shirt and the boots were part of it. The face behind the little moustache glowed with sweat and exertion and he wielded a steel fork and spatula with gusto. He was prodding and basting various cuts of meat that were sizzling on the grill. He didn't look like a real outdoorsman but he was giving it a brave try and obviously thought he was succeeding.

He saw me and waved. I moved closer but the wave had been perfunctory and he proceeded to ignore me, continuing to talk to the group around him. I was a bit annoyed, feeling I had been deliberately put in my place. True, I was just a junior audit manager and temporary at that, but he didn't have to rub it in. Someone with better manners – and without an axe to grind about low cost homes – would at least have said 'hi.'

I looked around the group. I only recognised two people. One was Dinesh Bosu and I didn't fancy talking to him. The other was the solid figure of Danie Basson, the builder of the Kloofdorp housing. At least he had been honest with me as far as I could tell, so I decided to go and greet him.

But as I was about to do so, someone called my name. It was Jerrie Naudé. He was sitting at one of the tables with Victor Mbutu and two women, presumably their wives. I went over.

Introductions were made. Jerrie's wife Annike was white, a blonde, with a friendly smile. Victor's wife Susie was black like her husband. Both women were good looking but Susie in particular was a knockout – slender, with hair piled high on top of her head and big silver earrings. She had a smooth skin and perfect features but her most striking attribute was an amused expression that caught and held my attention.

"Some interesting people here," I said. "A mixture of friends and enemies."

Jerrie raised an eyebrow and I immediately regretted my flippancy.

"Who are the enemies?" asked Victor mischievously.

I laughed. "I shouldn't have said that. Actually, I only recognise two people, our client Dinesh Bosu and the builder Danie Basson."

"Let me save you embarrassment," said Jerrie. "Here's a couple of folk for your rogues' gallery. See the big guy in the group by the grill, standing next to Dinesh?"

"The Indian-looking man?" I asked. He was large, six foot four and broad in proportion, with fierce bushy eyebrows. There was a long white scar on his brown cheek. Even in the noisy company I could hear his braying laugh at intervals.

"That's the guy."

"What did he do that's so bad?"

"He's a Bosu for starters – that is Haresh, the middle brother."

"You shouldn't speak disrespectfully about a client, should you?"

"Maybe not, but it's well known that in business he is a thief who never gives anyone an even break. There are also rumours of violence to his name."

"Is he the reason the Bosus have been so successful?"

"He and Shiv, his older brother and head of the family."

"Is Shiv here tonight?"

"I haven't seen him. He spends a lot of time rubbing shoulders with the high and mighty in Joburg and Pretoria. He and Haresh make an effective pair, one smooth, the other rough."

"There's another big fellow standing next to Haresh."

"That's Abel, his sidekick. South African, basically muscle. He's not too smart, just does whatever Haresh tells him."

"Maybe I'll go and take a closer look."

"Okay. Don't get too close."

"Why?"

"Trust me, it's not a good idea."

"But I need food, so I had better go and check out the grill." I looked at his plate. "What are you all eating?"

He waved his fork at what looked like some thick slices of sausage. "*Boerewors*. You have to try it."

"It's just sausage, right? They have steak there too, I like a good steak."

"This is not just any old sausage, man. This is ninety percent beef, a little bit of lamb, no cheap filling. Nothing like what you see in the supermarkets where you come from."

"Okay," I said reluctantly.

Victor's wife Susie chimed in. "Put some *mealie pap* on your plate to go with it."

"The stuff like grits? I don't care for grits, they don't have any taste."

She laughed. "You must add *Chakalaka*. That has plenty of taste."

"Excuse me?"

"*Chakalaka*. It's a thick sauce of tomatoes, beans, onions, garlic and a host of other stuff – chilis, curry, coriander. You'll see a big pot of it up there. Ladle some over the pap, it's a natural marriage."

So, obeying orders, I armed myself with an empty plate and approached the grill.

Boerewors turned out to be a sausage but coiled up in a spiral without links, like a Catherine wheel about a foot across. I asked the chef, who was assisting Van Biljon, to cut me a piece. Rather than trying to pronounce the word I just pointed at it, but I was more at home speaking the words 'pap' and '*Chakalaka*' and he grinned and spooned a dollop of each onto my plate.

As I turned away from the grill, balancing a beer can and a full plate, I came face to face with the three people I least wanted to talk to – Dinesh Bosu, Haresh Bosu and his stooge Abel.

17

Dinesh gave me an uneasy look, somewhere between welcoming and nervous. "Glad to see you enjoying our gastronomic culture," he said.

I wasn't feeling polite. "Your culture? Wouldn't that be goat curry and chapattis?" The more I thought about it, his collaboration with Van Biljon over the architects' fees was highly suspicious. Thirty-five million dollars is a lot of money by any standards.

I tried to walk past him, but he moved in my way.

"I want you to meet my brother, Haresh," he said.

We shook hands. When one sees a seriously disfigured person for the first time it can be hard to know where to look. Should one acknowledge the blemish or ignore it? Obviously ignoring is more diplomatic, but it can be difficult.

To avoid staring at the thin white scar running from his mouth to his ear, I looked him straight in the eye.

That presented another problem because his right eye was glass, and fixed. The good eye moved as he looked me up and down. The glass eye did not.

"Ah, Mr. Steele, I've been hearing about you."

"Really?"

"Yes indeed."

"What have I done?"

"You've asked a lot of questions."

"That's what auditors are supposed to do."

"So many questions can amount to inappropriate behaviour."

I shrugged. "Not really."

I moved aside, only to be faced by the solid bulk of Abel, as tall as Haresh and even broader. He didn't speak, he just stood there and scowled. I don't know if I was meant to feel scared, but what I actually felt was annoyed. I considered upending my beer over him but instead I took a deep breath, moved away and rejoined Jerrie and company at their table.

Jerrie had been watching. "What was all that about?"

"You tell me," I said. I addressed my dinner.

The *boerewors* was a gastronomic wonder. It bore only superficial resemblance to any sausage I was used to. The consistency was meaty, the taste rich and full-bodied – the beef and lamb flavours both came through, along with a hint of tarragon and other spices. The fragrance of the applewood on which it was grilled was the crowning touch. However much I disliked Van Biljon, I had to give him credit for only serving the best.

"This is excellent," I said.

"What did we tell you?" smiled Victor's wife Susie. "Try the *Chakalaka*."

I tasted it. "The perfect complement."

I sensed approval around the table.

The rest of the evening passed in pleasant conversation. I was particularly intrigued by a topic that I was hesitant to bring up, but I should not have worried because Susie raised it first.

"What do you make of what you've seen in South Africa so far?"

"In what sense?"

"The racial sense."

I was taken aback by her directness. She noticed my surprise, but she just laughed. "Come now, it's one of the things that make South Africa unusual – the combination of a black voting majority and a large, relatively affluent white minority. Not to mention several other ethnic groups thrown in for luck. Surely you can see why we're interested in how things look to an outsider."

"Okay," I conceded.

"What are your first impressions?"

I took a minute to frame my thoughts. "Since you bring it up, what struck me first was the general lack of self-consciousness between the races."

"What do you mean?" asked Victor. "What should we be self-conscious about?"

"I don't really know. But in some other countries there can be a certain edge when a white and a black person meet for the first time and have a discussion. In the United States, for instance, I sometimes sense that people are going out of their way to be extra polite in such situations."

Jerrie said, "I've not seen anything like that."

"That's what I'm saying. I don't see it in South Africa. People here are more natural."

"I know what he's talking about. I saw it in the States," said Susie.

"I didn't know you were there," I said.

She nodded. "I spent three years living in Connecticut."

"She has a master's degree in fine arts from Yale," said Victor proudly.

Susie said, "I suspect the African in the street just doesn't think about it. After all, it's been a quarter of a century since the first universal voting in 1994. I was only three at the time, so I've grown up not knowing anything different, like most young people. But South Africa does have some serious problems. You've heard of state capture?"

"I have indeed."

"State capture is a symptom of a much deeper socio-political malaise that arises, I'm sad to say, from black empowerment leading to widespread corruption, with officials and politicians using municipalities as their piggy banks."

I nodded. I had heard the same from Jasmine on my 'plane flight.

She went on. "I mentioned the affluent white minority but there are well-heeled blacks too, including a bunch who did not come by their wealth legally. As one journalist put it, South Africa today is like a cup of coffee. Not good strong Arabica coffee, more of a cappuccino – 80% black with a little cream on top representing the whites, and in that cream we have a few chocolate chips representing the rich blacks."

I said, "Here's another sensitive subject. What is the future of white-owned farmland? I was quite shocked when the President announced that he supported the takeover of those farms without compensation." I turned to Jerrie. "Most of that land belongs to Afrikaners. You're an Afrikaner, how do you feel?"

"It's disgraceful," interrupted his wife Annike. Her pretty brow wrinkled in anger.

Jerrie shook his head. "It won't happen," he said mildly.

"It happened in Zimbabwe, and look at the chaos it caused," she said crossly. "You're much too trusting."

Jerrie said, "The President did say that, but I don't think he really meant it. He was trying to make himself popular with African voters, ahead of a general election. And actually he only said he supported a change in the constitution that would permit the takeover of the farmland, which is unlikely to happen."

"Unlikely?" Anneke scoffed. "Sometimes you are so naive."

We were clearly on sensitive ground and I didn't want to disturb the Naudés marital harmony so I changed the subject.

After an hour or so the crowds thinned out and most people left. Jerrie and Victor got up to go home and I was following them out when Dinesh Bosu approached me with an ingratiating smile on his face and said, "Can we talk?"

I would have much preferred to leave with Jerrie and company, but Dinesh made that difficult by sitting down beside me.

"I hope we didn't get off too much on the wrong foot," he said.

I shrugged. "Doesn't bother me, I just do my job."

"As you should, of course." Again the mealy-mouthed smile. Or was I being unfair? It seemed churlish to object to a guy who was just trying to be polite.

"Danie Basson is a good man, a competent builder, but he doesn't understand the finer points of design. A lot of thought went into the design of that Kloofdorp housing. A lot of money too, but as we build more hous-ing, the cost will be amortised over a wider base."

I nodded. I had eaten well and consumed several beers and I wasn't really interested in arguing the toss this late at night. I just wanted to go home.

"How's your hotel?" he asked. "Everything good there?"

"It's fine." I looked at my watch.

"We could find you a better place. At our expense."

What was he babbling about? Yes it was his expense, it was common for a client to pay the accountant's out-of-pocket costs. I checked my watch again. "It's getting late."

"Sure." He stood up reluctantly.

We were the last to leave. The spotlights in the trees

had been turned off and so, to my surprise, had the lights in the house. As we walked back past the unlit building I had an uneasy feeling about being alone in the dark with him.

We reached the front of the house. The only cars left, either in the driveway or across the road, were mine and two others, one of which presumably was Dinesh's. Then I realised that the other one probably belonged to Haresh and the bodyguard Abel. Both of them were standing between me and my car.

18

The reason for Dinesh's friendliness was now clear. He had simply been delaying me until everyone else had left. I was now alone in the dark surrounded by three hostile individuals.

I nodded at Dinesh. "You tricked me."

He turned away, not meeting my eye.

I glanced back at the house. Interesting that it was dark. Van Biljon might be tucked up in bed fast asleep, but I doubted it. More likely he knew what might take place and wanted to be sure he had nothing whatever to do with it.

A bad scene. Should I call the police? To tell them what? That I didn't like the look of a couple of my fellow guests at the accountants' *braai*? And be laughed out of court?

∾

"So let us resume our chat," said Haresh. There was enough moonlight to make out his looming height and broad shoulders.

"You picked an odd moment for it," I said.

He shrugged. "No time like the present."

We were standing beyond the driveway, on the edge of the main road. The roads were quiet at that time of night, with little traffic. "Consider this your last chance," he said. "We need an auditor who will do what we pay him to do."

"Which is?"

"Approve a clean audit certificate, with no petty complaints about architects' fees or the allowability of picnic expenses, or anything else."

I sighed. "The trouble is, that's not how it works."

He laughed. "Maybe not in New York, or London, or wherever you come from. But this is not your territory, it's our territory. Here, we set the rules."

"We?"

"My brothers and I."

"There's something called the law of the land," I said gently.

He shook his head. "Things have changed in South Africa. This is frontier country now, my friend. Different rules apply."

"I'm not aware of a law to that effect."

"You seem to be obsessed with laws or rules or whatever you want to call them. The reality is different. That's what I'm trying to make clear to you. Nowadays, might is right."

He took a step towards me and I saw to my amazement that he held a tyre iron or heavy object in his hand. I moved back. I was not afraid of him, more like astonished. It was an unreal situation. I've dealt with angry clients in my accounting career, some of them potentially violent. But none have ever threatened me with a tyre iron. I guess there's a first time for everything.

But things didn't happen that way. The blow came from behind, a heavy punch to my neck. Not Dinesh, who was at his brother's side, so Abel the bodyguard. The roundhouse blow was so hard that I half lost consciousness.

I sensed myself being pushed out into the street where I collapsed on the roadway. I lay there, dizzy, desperately trying to understand what their plan was. In a moment it came to me. Sooner or later there would be traffic and my body was in the path of any oncoming car or truck. There would be a tragic 'accident' and it would all be over.

I could feel Dinesh and Abel hauling me upright. Headlights lightened the sky and I heard a vehicle approaching. They pulled me back to the edge of the road, out of its expected path.

Had I misunderstood? There was no plan to kill me, thank goodness. For a moment I felt relief.

That feeling lasted about two seconds. Then I realised this too was part of the plan. They were not going to leave me sprawled in the road at random. Of course not. An oncoming car would see my body and swerve. Instead, they would wait until the very last minute, when it was too late for traffic to change direction. That's when they would give me a good shove and leap back themselves.

The unseen vehicle approached, its noise louder. I was firmly in the grip of Dinesh on one side and Abel on the other.

There is a certain providence that looks after people in the situation I was in, the almost-victims. Call it instinct or maybe just panic. Call it whatever you like but it came to my rescue, thank God. What it did was clear my head. The mists receded. I was able to take stock of where I was, where we all were.

I don't think I am a brave person, in fact I'll go a long way to avoid physical violence. The last time something like this happened to me was in Cuba, when I was attacked at night in the grounds of the Hotel Magnifica by a renegade police chief with a gun. In the chaos the gun went off. It could have killed me but instead it killed him. Survival instinct or dumb luck? Who knows? But he is dead and I'm still here to tell the tale. For now, anyway.

The three of us stood on the grass verge outside Van Biljon's darkened house, facing back toward oncoming traffic. Dinesh gripped my left arm, Abel my right. Cars drive on the left hand side of the road in South Africa so, for a moment, Dinesh was closer to traffic than I was.

That's not why I pushed him. I did so because, of him and Abel, he was the weaker and my best chance of getting free. So it was Dinesh I shoved, with all my might.

He staggered back, releasing his grip on my arm and

losing his balance. There was only one direction he could go – straight into oncoming traffic.

The vehicle that hit him was a late model Audi A6, a solid German sedan with a reputation for being well put together. It had been travelling at perhaps forty miles an hour – not really speeding, but it was fast enough. Dinesh fell right into its path. Any change of direction was impossible, it was much too late.

Skid marks established later that the driver braked immediately and in a straight line. He was a white farmer driving home after having supper with neighbours. The first thing he did when the police arrived was to request a breathalyser test, which was sensible of him, I might have done the same in his position. The test proved negative. It protected him from liability and helped his insurance situation. The car's body was dented, the radiator cracked and the four-ring Audi motif on the front grille twisted and bloodstained.

The autopsy showed Dinesh's body to have a blood alcohol level of .10, slightly above the legal limit for driving. There is no legal limit for walking across the road. I had enjoyed a few drinks myself but it never became an issue.

19

The lights in the house came on and Van Biljon appeared, in his pyjamas. He claimed to have been asleep until the noise woke him.

There were genuinely shocked expressions of dismay, with Van Biljon muttering "Dreadful, dreadful!"

I was pretty shocked myself – there was no need for me to put on an act.

Even the stolid Abel was shaking. Only Haresh was unmoved, or appeared so.

The discussion with the police was mostly led by me.

"I guess he was crossing the road to get to his car," I said. "I think he'd had a bit to drink, quite honestly."

My version of events was not challenged by Haresh who was the only person in a position to do so since Abel took his cue from Haresh and Van Biljon had not been present.

The Audi had to be towed because of the broken

radiator. The police gave its driver a ride home. An ambulance took Dinesh's body to the morgue.

I drove back to my hotel alone. I would have felt bad about the whole thing except, heck, it was me they had planned to leave lying there, crumpled and lifeless on the road. Screw it!

20

Reactions to Dinesh Bosu's death varied widely. Within the family, his eldest brother Shiv came closest to displaying normal human sympathy. It had always saddened him that Dinesh, who was six years younger than he, had not shown more of an entrepreneurial spirit. But he was reconciled to the fact. He knew that Dinesh was who he was, and would not change. As a result, they got on well enough and had a calm and occasionally affectionate relationship.

So when Haresh told him about the events following the *braai*, Shiv's reaction was one of sadness as much as anything.

They were in Shiv's office, along with Basil Heinie.

Haresh was completely matter-of-fact. He told Shiv, "The boy stumbled. He was clumsy. That's all there is to say about it."

Shiv asked, "Who else was there last night?"

"Steele, the British accountant. And me, of course."

"What were you all doing?"

"Standing around talking, after the *braai*."

"Were you arguing?"

Haresh hesitated. "We may have been."

Shiv knew his brother and could put two and two together. A silence followed, broken by Haresh. "There was a scuffle."

Shiv said, his voice cracking, "Your use of violence risks undermining our whole position here. And it can go terribly wrong, don't you see that?"

Haresh shrugged. He was basically unmoved by Dinesh's death. The two had never had much in common, brothers or not. He was not going to cry over spilt beer.

Basil Heinie was watching them from across the room. He had no dog in the fight, not being fond of any of the three brothers. His contacts with Dinesh had been infrequent. He was privately amused by the indifference of Haresh, whom he considered to be a borderline psychopath, and the man's lack of empathy now only reinforced that opinion.

At least Heinie could not be accused of hypocrisy, since he made a virtue of being objective. He knew that his lack of warmth was considered an asset by Shiv who, while he did not like the South African, valued his judgement.

"With Dinesh's death we have nobody in charge over at Bosu Construction," Basil said.

Shiv nodded. "Haresh, you had better go over there

and act as manager until we can find someone permanent."

Haresh frowned. "Must I? I am not a house-builder."

"That's too bad," snapped Shiv. "We need someone there and it's a small sacrifice to make." It was a rare sign of anger. Haresh said nothing, but nodded assent, realising that his lack of sympathy for Dinesh might have gone too far.

21

The Protea Times reported Dinesh's death but it took second billing to the murder of another person with a connection to Protea, Lucy Gray. The headline said, "Accountant found dead."

Lucy's body had been found abandoned in the car park of a Hillbrow drugstore near her flat. She had been beaten and robbed. The cause of death was multiple blows to the head. Her purse was missing – she was only identified by a credit card receipt, a slip of paper in a pocket of her skirt, with her name on it.

Shiv summoned his brother. "I told you not to do that!"

Haresh shrugged. "We didn't mean to. She turned violent. Just a woman, but you would be surprised. Anyway, it solves a problem."

Shiv was furious. "No it doesn't. How long before some alert journalist notices that Gray was employed by LTH and checks to see if she worked on the Bosu audit?"

"But I bought you some time. That's what you said you wanted."

"Not like this."

"You need to be more decisive," said Haresh abruptly. "There is another issue facing us too, with Pelec and the Irish woman."

"Rebekka Moran?"

Haresh nodded. "Her report is due soon. If it criticizes us, that will be another blow."

"I'm aware of that."

"We should take care of her also."

Shiv shook his head. It was impossible to convey the concept of subtlety to Haresh.

But it was beyond dispute that things were getting critical. If Rebekka Moran implicated the brothers in another financial scandal, that could be a tipping point. Shiv was deeply uneasy about the speed at which events were unfolding. He was a man who liked to plan his life carefully, anticipating problems and taking steps to address them. But in recent days things had started to change too fast for him to enjoy that luxury. Something must be done. He sighed and looked at his watch.

"Well okay, deal with it. But no violence for god's sake."

"Sure." Haresh nodded reassuringly.

Shiv's voice rose. "I mean it." He marched out of the room.

Haresh grinned a fierce grin. His brother might be the clever one, the skilled executive with the suave manner, but at his core he was soft. It was a good thing he, Haresh, knew what it really took to get things done.

22

My telephone conversation with Carlton Tisch as he sat by his pool left me feeling uneasy. Carlton was one of those people who are much more interested in holding forth themselves than in listening to what you have to say. Sarcasm was wasted on him, it flowed straight over his head.

But events in Protea were disturbing. The attitude of the accountant Van Biljon and of the late Dinesh Bosu strongly suggested that their business ethics were non-existent and I was frankly relieved to be leaving for a weekend in Johannesburg.

~

"Welcome to Joburg," said Rebekka. We were at the airport, where she had offered to meet my plane.

"My boss Carlton says hi," I said.

"Thanks. I've not met him, but *my* boss says he's one

of the good guys. I guess they are drinking buddies on Wall Street." She grinned. "Above my pay grade."

She looked about my age. Shoulder length dark hair, pale complexion, her natural expression a half-smile. She was wearing a white silk blouse open at the neck. A black skirt and business-like dark stockings made her appear almost formal. Good looking, no doubt about it. Pearl necklace. No rings.

"Is it Joburg or Johannesburg?" I asked.

"That depends on your point of view."

"What's yours?"

"This is a brash business city – noisy, high energy, skyscrapers and freeways, dreadful traffic. A bit like Los Angeles."

"Sounds like a Joburg to me."

"Then we agree."

"Next question: where is your accent from? I'll guess Dublin."

She laughed. "Limerick."

"What brings you to this part of Africa?"

"Same thing as you, I imagine."

"Are you an accountant?"

"Management consultant."

"Carlton said you work for the Chicago Consulting Group. They have an excellent reputation."

"Which has been badly damaged here in South Africa."

"How so?"

"It's a long story."

We got into her car, a Toyota Camry. I moved a

squash racquet and sneakers off the passenger seat and tossed them in the back.

"Squash player?"

"Sort of."

"Any good?"

"Trinity College Dublin, third string. Ladies, of course. Yourself?"

"Oxford. Got a blue my last year."

"I'm impressed."

"It was a thin year."

"We should have a hit."

"Is there somewhere we can play?"

She laughed. "Joburg has some of the best sports facilities in the world. I play at the Wanderers, a great big club just north of town. What about this evening?"

"Good idea."

"Where are you staying?" she asked.

"I don't know yet. Any suggestions?"

"Why not try the Sunnyside Park Hotel. It's a bit old fashioned, but it has a nice garden. People like it."

So she drove us to the Sunnyside.

We had to talk our way past the uniformed guard at a security barrier. He was polite but thorough, recording the car's registration number and scanning my driver's license. He handed me a laminated pass, credit-card size. "Return this when you leave."

"Is that normal?" I asked Rebekka.

She nodded. "Yes, everywhere in Joburg, even the smart districts. This area, Parktown, is okay but you're close to some rougher places – Berea and Hillbrow. Better to be safe than sorry."

The Sunnyside was an attractive two-story Victorian building, long and low, built in the eighteen-nineties. It faced onto a leafy garden dominated by several massive plane trees whose spreading branches cast complex shadows on the lawn beneath. Broad stone steps led up to a dignified entrance and the lobby was panelled in dark wood. I noticed a comfortable lounge with deep armchairs and an elegant restaurant, its tables set with white tablecloths and gleaming silverware. My kind of place.

My bedroom was large and air conditioned. The shower head in the bathroom was one of those oversized contraptions a foot in diameter that deliver a scalding Niagara-like torrent.

~

Later that day I threw some kit in a bag, rented a car and drove to the Wanderers.

The club was set in spacious grounds in Ilovo, a white middle class area. The clubhouse was a large gabled building of somewhat jarring orange brick. Two flags fluttered in the breeze over the front portico – a South African banner and beside it the black and white Wanderers pennant featuring a chariot and rider reminiscent of Ben Hur.

Once again I had to explain myself to a security guard before he would allow me into to the car park. He scrawled a visitor pass for me to put on the dashboard. I met Rebekka in the clubhouse and we strolled down a slight slope past the cricket pitch and a dozen floodlit tennis courts, to the squash courts.

"Good trip so far?" she asked.

"Not sure yet."

"I booked the glass court," she said.

That was unexpected. In the old days squash courts had walls of solid white plaster. Only a handful of spectators could watch from an upstairs gallery which was just as well since most of us, even if we are decent club players, don't play like the top stars whose movement is a pleasure to watch.

We walked onto the floodlit court, its black floor marked with yellow lines. All four walls were of toughened glass and the ball was made of white rubber instead of the usual black. There was a gallery of about a hundred seats, all of them empty. I looked apprehensive.

"Don't worry," she laughed. "I doubt if we'll have an audience."

There were four other courts, but only one was in use. A middle aged white man was playing against a young black kid of not more than fifteen, possibly in a ladder match. Another African youngster was umpiring, calling the score impeccably.

I watched for a few minutes. The boy was cracking the ball up and down the side walls like a pro, with a teenager's inexhaustible energy. He was losing 10-3 when I arrived but he must have been loitering because he then won eight points in a row and went on to take the game 16-14. The white guy looked completely exhausted.

Rebekka was a useful player. She hit the ball harder than most women and had an ability to step back to the middle of the court between strokes that kept her in the rallies. But I had more experience and a stronger arm. I was able to dictate play and won the first game 11-5.

So I was taken by surprise when she increased her speed dramatically in the second game and won it 11-6.

"You upped the tempo there," I commented.

She just smiled. She maintained her pace and took the third game 11-0.

I was mortified. With my back to the wall I tried hard, but her relentless speed wore me down and I was breathing heavily as she went ahead 9-0 in the fourth. I can't be sure, but I think she eased up and let me win a couple of points toward the end. She still won 11-3, making the score 3-1 in games.

That was enough for me. I was breathing in huge gasps as we sat on the bleachers.

"How did you get so fit?" I wanted to know.

She laughed.

"It's not me, it's you. There are 5,800 good reasons why you found it such hard going."

I looked puzzled, then light dawned. "Altitude?"

"Exactly. We're on the High Veld, a plateau at 5,800 feet. That's higher than Denver at 5,300 although nowhere near La Paz, Bolivia at 11,800 feet. No wonder you're tired. You probably didn't notice it in the office, but playing a hard game of squash the day after an eleven hour plane journey is pushing it, too."

Over a Black Label in the bar, she said, "We're working on similar projects. You know that, don't you?"

"Carlton mentioned it."

She nodded. "My firm got into a bit of a mess. We're trying to clean it up ourselves before our professional body steps in and bans us from doing business in South Africa for good."

"Define *a bit of a mess*."

She pointed at my half-empty glass. "This could take a while."

She spoke concisely, but the situation she described was complex:

"Chicago Consulting was brought in to design a purchasing system for Pelec, the electrical utility company of the province of Protea. The idea was to ensure fair competition."

"Sounds worthy."

"As part of the deal, our fee – a stiff one – depended on the new system actually saving money."

I raised an eyebrow. "Do management consultants often operate based on results – on the come, so to speak?"

She hesitated. "It's a bit unusual. It's becoming more common, though."

"Go on."

"Well it looks as if that fee will never be paid."

"What went wrong?"

"With a view to designing the best possible system,

we sought help from outside contractors. The idea was to respect local conditions. Unfortunately, the contractor we used, Axton Solutions, turned out to have a major conflict of interest."

"I can guess what's coming. It's owned by a supplier to Pelec?"

"Yes. Axton is controlled by a firm that mines and sells coal. They wrote some language into the small print requiring that the successful candidate be incorporated in Biko City. This eliminated all the other candidates."

"And Chicago Consulting didn't read the small print?"

"That's not entirely clear."

"Meaning?"

"They may have read it and decided to ignore it."

"You mean Chicago Consulting collaborated in the deception?"

"Yes. One of their Joburg staff, anyway."

"But why?"

She shrugged. "They were bribed."

"That's a shocking thing to say about a prestigious outfit like Chicago Consulting."

She nodded. "I guess standards in some regional offices may not match those of our parent. Guess who owns Axton, by the way?"

"The Bosu family?"

"And Axton's auditors are?"

"LevyTeagardenHooper?"

Our eyes met.

She nodded drily. "Welcome to Joburg."

Tell me about the Bosus," I asked.

She nodded. "They are pretty big."

"How big?"

"Thousands of employees and a net worth in the billions."

"How long have they been around?"

"About five years."

"So recent? They must have been doing something dramatic to grow so fast."

"State capture can happen quickly."

"State capture? That's the term the stewardess on my plane used. What exactly does it mean?"

"It starts with bribery."

"Can you be more specific?"

"Okay. Five years ago, Bosu was just an importer of electrical generators from Japan, selling them here. Pretty humdrum."

"Profitable?"

"Moderately. Their breakthrough came one fine day when they sold a generator to Tom Maputo, Protea's Minister of Finance, for his private house."

"Why would he need one?"

She laughed. "Power cuts are a feature of life around here. Anyway, the Minister met Shiv Bosu, head of the Bosu clan, and they struck up a friendship."

"I've heard that Shiv is the diplomatic brother."

She nodded. "Anyway, the Minister never did pay for his new generator."

"Let me guess. Nor for anything else?"

"You've got the idea. 'Anything else' includes a tennis court, a bowling alley and an entire guest wing added onto his house. Oh, and he drives a brand new Jaguar. Not bad for a humble local politician on a modest salary paid from the public purse."

"Presumably there was a tradeoff. What did Bosu get in return?"

"A contract to supply coal to Pelec, Protea's government-owned electricity supplier. Pelec operates power stations, which generate electricity, which is then supplied to the long suffering customer."

"Long suffering?"

She laughed. "Power cuts are frequent. They affect homes and businesses. They even cause traffic jams, because Pelec supplies power to robots."

"Robots?"

"That's what they call the traffic signals here."

"So, the Bosu group: you said thousands of people?"

"Including employees. But you need only worry about four individuals – three, now that Dinesh is dead."

"I thought there were two remaining brothers, Shiv and Dinesh?"

"There is also Basil Heinie."

"Who?"

"Heinie is the missing piece. He completes the group. He is South African, an accountant in his fifties. He has been with the Bosus ever since they arrived from India. Heinie is smart, and highly driven. He is analytical and precise where the brothers are entrepreneurial. He also seems to be full of resentment against the government and against society in general. A very bitter character."

"For what reason?"

Rebekka shrugged. "He just seems to be made that way. He is coloured, not that that explains anything. Coloured folk are people just like anyone else. But they were badly treated under apartheid and in his case he has made that the excuse for all kinds of bitterness, which he is now taking out on the government, helped by the Bosus."

I probably looked ignorant, because I was. "You'll have to explain some terms. What exactly do you mean by coloured?"

"Let me simplify a bit. Under apartheid there were four main groups: black, white, Indian and coloured. Coloured can include Malays and Chinese but more often means there is some African blood. Heinie is light skinned but his grandfather was Zulu, from Natal. He grew up in the area near Cape Town known as District 6, a lively community of mostly coloured people speaking Afrikaans as their first language. In 1964 the Afrikaner government of Prime Minister Verwoerd decided to clear the whole area and re-designate it as white. Over ten years, 60,000 people were forcibly relocated to a miserable place called Cape Flats, 25 kilometres away, mostly sand and scrub. Just an all-around wretched thing to do. Heinie was a teenager at the time."

"So he hates whites? I can understand that. But why blacks?"

"Blacks are now the voting majority. The African National Congress, the party of Nelson Mandela and his fellow freedom fighters, has been in government for a quarter of a century. I suppose Heinie feels he is neither one thing nor the other.

"Anyway, he studied accounting at the University of the Western Cape, which in those days was a university for coloured people although it is now fully integrated, and applied for various government jobs without success. He was finally hired by Bosu. There was a meeting of minds – both Heinie and Shiv, for different reasons, want to stick it to the government financially. Before long Shiv Bosu promoted him to group chief accountant. Many of Shiv's state capture tactics were probably suggested by Heinie."

"So Heinie and the Bosus are united in efforts to steal from the South African government?"

"Yes, and not just South Africa. The same techniques of state capture – identifying susceptible leaders, bribing them and then stealing from state owned companies –

occur elsewhere including Zimbabwe and, potentially, Guinea-Malia."

"I know about Zimbabwe's problems, but why Guinea-Malia? I thought it was a stable country."

She shrugged. "I don't know all the details, but they have a head of state who is getting on in years and may be mildly senile. Heinie has been up there doing his best to cause trouble."

24

"**O**ne more person is key in all this," said Rebekka. "Tom Maputo."

"And he is?"

"Protea's Minister of Finance."

"He's the guy the Bosus bribed?"

She nodded.

"What's he like?" I asked.

"He's a personable chap, articulate and witty. Oxford educated. Only forty years old. All set for a bright future in national government, maybe even prime minister, except for one fatal flaw: he's a gambler."

"Big amounts?"

"Oh yes. He's addicted. The Bosus know it, in fact he frequents their tables. The word is he's into Joburg Casino for a six figure sum."

"That must make him very susceptible."

"Of course. It's because he is so firmly under the thumb of the Bosus that they can negotiate these lucrative deals with Pelec. He owes the Bosus so much that they sometimes let him win, just to keep him coming back. So he's being both blackmailed and bribed. It's quite a sick situation."

"How long has this been going on?"

"Several years. But it's only now, with the scale of Bosus' profits becoming known thanks to an aggressive financial press, that the public is learning about their goings-on. The Bosus have finally over-reached themselves."

"So Maputo must be heading for exposure and possibly disaster. Does he know it?"

"Hard to say. There are more and more press reports questioning the relationship. He still pals around with Shiv Bosu, the head of the family. To me that virtually proves there's some funny business going on, what with Shiv being the kind of person he is."

I took a long sip of beer.

"Can you prove all this?"

"The proof is coming."

"Real documentary proof?" I didn't want to offend Rebekka but I needed to know.

She nodded. "I'm working with our computer people in Chicago and they are obtaining – through unofficial channels – a download of several years of Axton emails. It includes messages sent by Maputo that will prove his complicity beyond a doubt."

"You are hacking into Axton's records? Is that legal?"

"Sometimes one has to fight fire with fire."

I was a bit taken aback by that, but her pretty face was expressionless.

"I suppose it's okay if it supplies a key piece of the puzzle." I was revising my opinion of Rebekka. Tougher than she looked. But her performance on court should have told me.

She looked pleased at the comment. "Yep!"

25

At the same time that Rebekka was describing Tom Maputo to Oliver, a meeting was beginning in a church hall in Biko City, sponsored by the local branch of the African National Congress, the ANC.

The secretary stood to introduce the guest speaker.

"We are honoured tonight to welcome Protea's distinguished Minister of Finance, Tom Maputo."

Applause.

"We all know of the Minister's gallant work for freedom in the years before the 1994 election and the coming of democracy."

Maputo listened gravely, his face a blend of modesty and pride.

"His brave support of President Mandela in those difficult years was a key part of our struggle."

That was not completely untrue, but it would have been more accurate to point out that at the time of the election Maputo was only twenty years old. He had joined the ANC in his teens and had only ever spoken a few words to Mandela. That had happened when the great man came to address the college where Maputo was a student.

But it was helpful for an ambitious black politician to have a link with the movement's past and to stress it for all he was worth. Most of his audience were too young to remember that the last white president, Frederik de Klerk, had progressively relaxed apartheid in the eighties in the face of international pressure, ending the ban on the ANC in 1990. So although Maputo was a loyal party member he had not really done much struggling.

He got to his feet. In his well cut suit he did not look like a freedom fighter but the audience did not care. A hero was a hero.

He gave a carefully rehearsed twenty minute speech in which he paid tribute to Nelson Mandela, Albert Luthuli, Walter Sisulu and other icons of the past. Being a thoughtful politician he took care also to mention Denis Goldberg, the only white member of ANC to be arrested and sentenced to life in prison for supporting the anti-apartheid movement. He went on to paint a brief but glowing picture of the future, promising free education and free medical treatment for all, and sat down to loud applause.

He then spent ten minutes smiling and shaking hands with members of the audience. One had to be a people person.

But he had other things on his mind. As soon as he

got outside he jumped in his Jaguar and drove to the Joburg Casino. He received a respectful nod from the security people there who knew him well and waved him in, and sat down to play poker.

He signed an IOU for chips worth a thousand dollars, a privilege not available to the general public, and lost most of the thousand within half an hour. He was about to ask the dealer for more when he felt an arm on his well tailored shoulder. It was Haresh Bosu.

"Ah, I was going to come and see you in a minute," said Maputo.

"Cards not falling your way?" laughed Bosu. "Not much we can do about that, I'm afraid."

"No, there's something else."

He got up and the two men went and sat at a quiet table in the corner of the Indian restaurant.

"I'm worried," said Maputo.

"So am I, but you know what? I never let it affect my appetite." Bosu pushed a menu at him.

The waiter brought their orders, prawn curry for Bosu and chicken tikka for Maputo. Bosu tore off a piece of garlic nan and used it to scoop up the fragrant sauce.

"Delicious. We brought the chef in from Mumbai." He smacked his lips. "Now, what's the problem?"

"It's the woman Moran."

"Ah yes, Rebekka. Good looking girl. How's her investigation going? I trust you're giving her as little help as possible."

"You can joke, but it's serious."

"How so?"

"She wants to know all about how Pelec buys its raw materials, particularly coal."

"A fair request."

"She's asked to see any emails between Axton and myself relating to the new purchasing system, the one designed by her colleagues from Chicago Consulting."

"That's the system where Pelec excludes applicants not registered in Biko City?"

"Exactly."

"I don't have to tell you how to respond. Be selective. If anything is embarrassing, hold it back. Is there any sensitive stuff there?"

"Yes. An exchange of emails in which Axton spelled out the Biko City condition. They quote the entire paragraph, and the reason for it. It's a smoking gun."

Bosu laughed. "Is that all? Delete the whole exchange. Make sure your IT guys delete it from the trash file, too."

Maputo shook his head. "I don't like it."

"What could go wrong?"

"She's also working with Chicago Consulting's own IT people. It seems they have a way of hacking directly into Pelec's database."

Bosu frowned. "From outside? How can they do that?"

Maputo looked glum. "How should I know? One can do anything with computers nowadays."

"Has she given the order to Chicago yet?"

"I don't think so. But she will, any day."

Bosu glanced at Maputo's plate. The African had hardly touched his food.

"Eat up, it's delicious," said Bosu. He spooned saffron rice onto his plate to mop up the curry and took a large mouthful. "You know what? Young Rebekka may have to be neutralised."

"Neutralised?"

"Made to go away."

"She won't go away. She has a job to do, and she's very determined."

"You don't understand. When I say go away, I mean she must disappear."

Maputo finally got Haresh's meaning. He looked doubtful.

"That's too extreme. Besides, I have no way to make it happen."

"You don't have to make it happen. I will handle it. Just do nothing."

He glanced sideways at Maputo. *You're another one like my brother,* he thought. *Smooth, a good politician. But when push comes to shove, you've got no guts.*

"I'll fix it. Leave everything to me." He glanced at Maputo's half-full plate. "Are you going to finish that curry?"

"I'm not really hungry."

Bosu reached across and slid Maputo's plate towards him.

26

I was at a loose end. There was nothing more I could do for now, so I called Rebekka. It was not as if I knew a lot of people in Joburg.

"How about a return match."

She laughed. "My advice? Give it a few days. If I beat you again you'll never get over it and I'm not sure I want that responsibility."

"Fair enough. What about a drink somewhere?"

"Do you like to gamble?" asked Rebekka.

"Not really."

"There are several casinos in Joburg," she said. "And the night is young."

I let the remark hang. She obviously wanted to go gambling whether I liked the idea or not.

"The biggest place, Joburg Casino, is owned by our friends the Bosus," she said. "Maybe you should take a look, learn who you're dealing with?"

"Fair enough. Pick you up in twenty minutes?"

Joburg Casino was on the north side of downtown, not far from the Zoo. It was a massive place. The attached hotel had two hundred rooms. Outside, huge fountains resembling those at the Bellagio in Las Vegas swirled to and fro and played soft music. But the dominant feature was the six life-sized gold lions that leaped out through the water plumes, aggressive and challenging.

A scarlet neon sign glowed overhead in the rapidly cooling evening air as we approached in Rebekka's Toyota.

We headed for the tables but were prevented, as usual, by security – this time two uniformed Africans, a man and a woman. The man ran his electronic wand over me while the woman did the same to Rebekka. Only then were we allowed to proceed onto the gaming floor.

"I see you're getting used to Joburg security," she said.

I waved a hand, palm downwards in a gesture of 'maybe.'

In order to get to the gaming area we had to pass through an elegantly decorated lobby panelled in dark wood. A full-size portrait of a dignified looking gentleman in a Nehru jacket hung on one wall, illuminated by a spotlight. The gilt frame bore a label saying 'Vikram Bosu, 1890-1972.'

"Who's that?" I asked Rebekka.

"I think it's an ancestor of the owners, Shiv and his brothers. Maybe the casino is dedicated to him."

"He looks an honorable man."

She laughed. "He does. Whether his good qualities were passed down to the present generation of Bosus is another question."

The main gaming room was huge, on the Las Vegas scale. It was only moderately busy. The blackjack tables were quiet. But one big difference from most of the United States was the existence of a smoking section – a big one. That was where the real action was, with roulette tables and plenty of blackjack. Hundreds of slot machines rattled and screeched deafeningly. Roulette was going on with hundred rand chips. The crowd seemed to consist mainly of Africans, obviously enjoying themselves, with a sprinkling of what looked like European tourists.

"I haven't eaten all day, I'm ravenous," said Rebekka.

"Let's go and eat then."

There were several restaurants, including an Indian and a Portuguese, as well as a buffet. A food court offered more choices, with a Kentucky Fried Chicken, a Debonairs Pizza shop and some other stands.

We decided on the buffet.

We talked as we ate. Rebekka was enquiring and insightful and I could see why she was well regarded by her firm. I found myself telling her more about my exploits than I usually share with strangers.

Maybe it was the alcohol, but I started to talk about the killings I've been involved with. Shooting people can make a mess of your emotions, even though it's something I've had to do several times now. At first it made me feel guilty and somehow unworthy. Never mind that my adversaries were killers themselves and the scum of the earth, which they certainly were, I had taken life. It was not a good feeling. That was bad enough, but after a while I began to feel differently about the act itself. There was a sense of being above the law, of being my own law even. The mood crept in against my wishes, but in a disturbing way I enjoyed it. I did not share that with her.

After several drinks, there was a pause. Rebekka looked embarrassed.

"There's something I want to ask."

"Go ahead."

"It may offend you."

"Takes a lot."

"Okay. Are all accountants so lacking in passion, so matter of fact?"

I could read her mind, at least I thought so. She was thinking, 'He gets into these crazy situations, barely escapes with his life and still doesn't seem to engage emotionally. I want to like him, to cheer for him, but...'

"It's a fair question." I was trying to buy some time.

"I keep hoping Oliver Steele will prove he's not made of steel after all."

"I've had some meaningful romantic encounters," I said.

"But do you expose your heart? I suspect not."

We had only just met and already she was psycho-analysing me? I tried to feel annoyed, but in fact she was right. I do find it hard to talk about emotions. Friends say that I have no feelings because I don't get attached to any of the good looking women I bump into, but that's not true. I have feelings, it just takes a while to get around to showing them.

"Fine," I said. "You're right and I'm wrong. Can we change the subject?"

She shrugged. "If you insist." She thought for a minute. "Next question: don't you ever get scared?'

"Of course I do."

"How do you handle that?"

"With difficulty. It's not as though I was in the military. I did not choose a job where violence is normal, it was thrust upon me so to speak. A soldier can probably pull the trigger without emotion. A fighter pilot can fire on a hostile plane and not worry about the poor sap he sends crashing down in flames. But in my case I struggle with doubts whenever it happens."

"Which seems to be often."

"When I'm working for Tisch, yes. I spend a lot of time grubbing around in the ethical mud while he sits in the sun or sails his bloody yacht round Tortola!"

She had touched a nerve and I was getting animated. When I became an accountant I thought I was set for life. I enjoyed the work, liked dealing with numbers. I was ready for a successful, non-violent professional career. But it didn't turn out that way.

So there you are, that's Oliver Steele. Smiling and calm on the outside. Inside, full of resentment. It was a lot to try and explain to Rebekka and it didn't sound entirely convincing, even to me.

"If you get to know me better you may detect a few traces of emotion," I said.

"Go ahead, joke about it." She sounded testy.

Or was I the testy one?

I looked at my watch. "Let's go and check out the tables."

~

Rebekka led me to a blackjack table, looking excited. In no time she was seated with a pile of chips in front of her. Free cocktails arrived.

I estimated her chips were worth five hundred dollars. Where did she get the money? I never take more than two hundred into a casino and when I lose it, I leave. Unromantic, I know, but you do always lose in the end.

Rebekka burned through most of her chips in about an hour. The cards shook in her hands as she sat in front of the dealer and her pretty face grew pink as she focused intently on each card dealt. Most decisions in blackjack involve following a few simple rules, so her emotional commitment seemed a bit excessive and I couldn't help wondering if she had an addictive personality.

I was afraid she would lose the rest of her stake in minutes, but I was able to prise her away in time. She was a bit unsteady and I had to steel myself to get in her car and allow myself to be driven back to my hotel.

"I'll show you the good and the bad of Joburg on the

way," she said. She drove for a few minutes, then stopped by the side of the road and pointed to a high circular building ahead.

"That's Ponte City, where your unfortunate Lucy Gray had her flat."

It was an immense cylindrical tower. I know it's a cliché to describe a building as a phallic symbol but in this case the description seemed apt. The structure was tall and slender, its fifty floor height many times its width. It stood on a broader base of several circular floors of parking. Its tip was several floors high, bright red and sporting a neon advertisement for the phone company Vodacom.

"It's a building that illustrates rather well what this city has become."

"What do you mean?"

"Democracy is a wonderful thing. Apartheid was dreadful – the lack of freedom, absence of free speech, relocation of minorities when it suited the white government. The torture and death of heroes, a few of them famous and many others whose names will never be known. It was horrible."

"Clearly," I said.

But she hadn't finished.

"However, democracy brought some side effects. One of which was white flight."

"Did that happen to Ponte City?"

"With a vengeance. It consisted originally of elegant apartments with spectacular views, but in a few years it was a total mess, riddled with gangs and prostitution.

The central courtyard was piled several floors high with trash – when they cleared it they found dead animals and, according to rumour, human remains."

"Is it still that way?"

"No. After several failed attempts it has finally been cleaned up and security tightened. A few young professionals like Lucy Gray have moved in, attracted by the low rents." She laughed. "I still think it's an eyesore but that's just my opinion."

"Which I share," I said.

"Now I'll show you something else shocking." She swerved back onto the surface street.

"Where are we going?"

"To what used to be beautiful downtown Joburg."

We drove a couple of miles and she stopped in front of another massive high-rise building, dark against the navy blue sky. There was a thin moon and in front of the skyscraper I could see a plaza surrounded by other buildings.

"What do you make of this?" she said.

We got out. She strolled a few yards and I followed her.

"Looks like an office building," I said. "No lights. I guess the workers have gone home."

"No, that's not the case. This is the Central Business District and that" – she waved an arm – "used to be the Carlton Hotel. This whole development was a handsome, sophisticated place, a bit like the Rockefeller Center in Manhattan. It even had an ice rink."

"Are you saying it is closed?"

She nodded. "It's a symbol of how things have gone downhill since universal suffrage. In 1993, Nelson Mandela held his seventy-fifth birthday celebration at the hotel, but crime got progressively worse and people just stopped coming here. In 1997, two hotel employees murdered an assistant manager who caught them drinking on duty and hid his body in the hotel's linen room. They got twenty-three years in jail. The hotel closed later that year."

"You're not opposed to votes for everyone, are you?" I asked.

"Of course not. But something's not working and that's a fact."

There was a crashing sound behind us. We swung round.

A truck stood near Rebekka's car. It had apparently side-swiped it. Two figures loomed in front of us, just outlines in the darkness but obviously large and male. One of them wrapped his arms around Rebekka and swept her roughly aside.

I grabbed her attacker and drew back a fist to hit him. Both my hands were grabbed from behind and I stumbled and lost my balance.

And that's all I remember for a while.

27

Wen I recovered, the moon was still in the
same place so I reckoned that I was only
unconscious for a few minutes.

I was flat on my back on the sidewalk. My head
throbbed abominably. I reached under my hair and felt a
tender area the size of a hundred rand poker chip.

I sat up slowly and checked my pockets – my wallet
and phone were still there. I could see Rebekka's car a
few feet away. But of Rebekka, no sign.

I used my phone to Google "Police," and got a phone
number. When they replied I explained, "I've been
robbed, and my friend kidnapped."

"Where are you, sir?"

I was flustered and could not explain immediately,
but I was able to switch to Google Maps and find my
position using the little blue dot on the screen. Then I
remembered.

"I'm near the Carlton Centre."

"Is your car working?"

"It's her car, not mine."

Yes, sir," patiently. "See if you can start it."

I tried and the motor rumbled into life. "Okay."

"Better come here, to the central police station."

"Which is where?"

"Number 1, Commissioner Street. Five minutes' drive."

I fed the address into Google Maps and in moments I was there.

The police station was a glass and steel high-rise building with blue walls. I had to talk my way past a dour desk sergeant in the open-necked shirt of SAPS, the South African Police. Then I waited for ten minutes on a hard chair in an interview room about as welcoming as a prison cell. Finally, a young man in plain clothes entered and sat opposite me.

"Sorry, we're short staffed. I'm detective Fourie. What's the problem?"

I explained that Rebekka had disappeared.

"What were you doing in that part of town?"

"She was showing me the Carlton Hotel."

"Why would she do that? It is closed."

"That was the point."

"I don't understand."

"I'm a visitor to South Africa. She was explaining what has happened to Johannesburg in recent years."

I bit my tongue, afraid I would sound offensive, but he did not seem to mind. He half-smiled. "We've had our issues."

He turned serious again. "I'll take the information, then we'd better go and have a look."

He beckoned constable Luthuli, a huge uniformed African with a ready smile. Back to the Carlton Centre, but there was little to see. Luthuli swept the scene with a flashlight, coming to rest on the tyre tracks of a vehicle, not Rebekka's. "Did you see what kind of car it was?" he asked.

"It was a truck, and grey. But it was dark, and I don't know vehicle makes very well. When I was a kid I could identify most of them but today they all look the same."

"I know what you mean. My teenage sons recognise everything." He pointed the flashlight at the side of Rebekka's car. The bodywork was crumpled and showed streaks of grey paint.

He scraped off some chips of the paint with a penknife and tipped them carefully into a small polythene bag which he put in his pocket.

Then he took some photos. "Is this a rental?"

"Yes. She's here on a job."

"I hope she bought the full insurance."

～

Back in my room at the Sunnyside I phoned Carlton again. It was ten pm in Joburg, four pm on Tortola.

"What's up?" he asked.

"Bad news." I explained about the death of Lucy Gray and the disappearance of Rebekka.

"Do you think she's dead too?" he asked.

"I don't know. I hope not."

"What can I do to help?" asked Tisch.

"Not much. You're too far away. I just wanted to vent."

"I have a friend in Johannesburg," he said. "He's pretty resourceful."

"I'll take any help I can get. What's his background?"

"He's in mining, on the financial side. His name is Harvi, Rod Harvi. We've done a few deals together."

Carlton usually understates the facts when it comes to money, so I assumed the deals had a good few zeros on the end. But if Harvi was another investor like Carlton I didn't see how he could be much help. What I really needed was a combination of detective and strong-arm man, with a nose for tracking down missing persons.

But I didn't want to discourage Carlton. "Give me his phone number."

"I don't have it here. I'll get him to call you."

I suddenly felt tired. Walking across the room to fetch a glass of water, I staggered and almost passed out.

"Not tonight," I said. "I'm bushed. Tomorrow."

Luckily the beds at the Sunnyside were excellent.

∼

At seven next morning the phone rang.

"Mr. Steele?" The accent was precise, more eastern European than South African.

"Speaking."

"Rod Harvi."

"Ah. Thanks for calling. Let's see, how can I explain."

"No need. We should meet." Brisk.

"Where is your office and how do I get there?"

"You don't. I'll send a car. You're at the Sunnyside?"

"Yes."

"Be ready in twenty minutes."

I was mildly irritated. I hadn't had my first cup of coffee. But he sounded efficient and I had no other irons in the fire.

"Got it," I said, trying to match his rapid-fire manner.

~

In the car I noticed we were heading north, in the opposite direction from the scene of last night's drama.

"Where are we going?" I asked the driver.

"To Head Office."

"Whose head office?"

He frowned – a foolish question. "JGM's."

JGM, Johannesburg Global Mining, was one of the biggest and best known mining groups in the world. It was a leading miner of gold, iron, coal, platinum and diamonds. It was founded by Solly Wertheim, a Jewish immigrant to South Africa, in 1920 so its centenary was approaching.

"Does Harvi work there?"

"Sir Rod is our chairman."

Oops. Luckily I was wearing a jacket and tie.

After a fifteen minute drive we approached a cluster of futuristic office buildings, much newer and a whole lot cleaner than the Carlton Centre. "Where are we?" I asked.

"This is Sandton, which many people call the new business capital of Africa." He pointed to a slender tower reaching halfway into the clouds. "That's the Leonardo Tower. When it opens in a few months it will outstrip the Carlton Centre as the tallest building in Africa."

JGM's headquarters building was a gleaming steel structure, a curved-sided rhomboid standing on end. Etched across its huge glass entrance were the words, "Johannesburg Global Mining South Africa," an indirect reminder that the company was legally based in London. Its shares were quoted on the London Stock Exchange with a secondary listing in Johannesburg. I owned a few JGM shares before I went broke. Its original mines were in South Africa, but it now owned a string of mines and mineral concessions around the world in various stages of development.

Rod Harvi's office was on the top floor. The carpet was thick up there among the gods and the windows stretched from floor to ceiling. There was a panoramic view across the city. Front and centre was the Leonardo skyscraper my driver had pointed out. It looked as if it was on the very point of completion. Harvi's secretary, a middle aged woman with a sensible manner, saw me looking at it.

"It was designed by a South African architect," she said. "The reason it's so narrow is that it's built on the foundations of another building that was there before."

Harvi's office door was closed. "He says his door is always open except when it's shut," she smiled.

"Will he be long?"

"He's on a conference call, so it may take a while. Here's something to read while you're waiting – our annual report."

I sat down and flipped to the financial pages. The profit and loss account showed US$12.4 billion. At first I thought that was the company's sales but on looking closer I realised it was bottom line profit.

I turned to the balance sheet. The group was heavily indebted. I was working my way through the footnotes – that's usually where the real bodies are buried – when I became aware of a figure standing in front of me.

He held out a hand. "Rod Harvi."

He was older than me, probably in his sixties. Medium height and a little chubby round the middle. Not intimidating, not the sharp mannered type Carlton Tisch usually hung out with. More grandfatherly. But if I learned one thing when I worked in the City of London, there is no such thing as a 'type' when it comes to successful entrepreneurs.

I shook the offered hand.

He indicated the annual report. "That's a year old. A lot has changed since then."

"JGM has a lot of debt," I said.

He shook his head. "Not any more. We recently sold a lot of our coal mines, got out of copper entirely and reduced payroll from 130,000 to 80,000 people."

Not grandfatherly at all.

"I'm impressed."

"So is the stock market. Our shares have doubled in the last year. Now then, I had a text message from Carlton saying you needed help. No details. What can I do for you?"

I explained Carlton's interest in Bosu Construction, and how, following my meeting with Paul Coward in London, I had flown to Joburg to investigate.

"Things have taken a nasty turn," I said. "First the housing site turned out to be as bogus as hell. Then Lucy Gray, Bosu's auditor, was murdered. And now the kidnapping of Rebekka."

"Do you know her well?" he asked.

"No, we only just met. But we're both looking into situations involving the Bosu brothers that are turning out to be even more dubious than we expected. So there are similarities in our work. And we played squash together."

"What have you done to find her?"

"I went to the police, but they seem a bit overwhelmed. I don't know how much effort they'll put into the investigation."

He nodded. "Crime is a problem in Joburg. Here at JGM we don't put a lot of faith in the police, between you and me."

"That's quite a statement."

He shrugged. "We tend to rely on our own resources."

"What do you mean?"

"JGM is the equivalent of a small country. We have assets all over the world. We have to protect what we have, so we maintain our own security force. We also have extensive support facilities – research, scientific and so on."

"Here in Joburg?"

"Or within easy reach."

"Are you saying that you take the law into your own hands?"

He shrugged. "Sometimes."

I had a thought. "The constable scraped some paint samples off the side of Rebekka's car, where it was hit."

"We can have those analysed."

"That may be difficult. The police have them."

Rod smiled. "I doubt if they have the time or the skill to do much with them."

He called to his secretary. "Hilda, see if you can get Teddy Malongo on the phone."

"Who is that?" I asked.

"He runs the police here in Joburg."

A few minutes later, Hilda called, "The commissioner is on the line."

"Put him through," said Harvi. "Teddy, long time no see."

He listened. "My putting is dreadful too, yours can't be any worse."

More sounds from the phone.

"Nine holes this afternoon? At Woodmead? Perfect."

He rang off and looked at me. "Leave it with me. I'll call you."

28

J ohannesburg boasts some outstanding golf courses. Woodmead, which belongs to the Johannesburg Country Club, is arguably the finest. The course is dramatic, the clubhouse magnificent. The only problem is the unpredictable traffic on the De Villiers Graaff Motorway, the road you have to take to get there, Woodmead being twelve miles away from the Club's main premises in Auckland Park.

Rod Harvi booked the tee time for himself and a guest, since Malongo was not a club member. The Club would probably have been happy to welcome the police commissioner but he never applied, not wanting to spoil his carefully honed image as a man of the people. He grew up in Soweto and his parents still lived there, although in a better class section near the houses of such luminaries as Archbishop Desmond Tutu and the late Nelson Mandela. It was a useful status thing to keep your Soweto connection if you had one.

Harvi got to the golf club half an hour before their 2 pm reservation. He took his time putting on his golf shoes in the spacious locker room, then had a cappuccino at the outdoor coffee bar, but he was still waiting as 2 o'clock came and went.

Finally, at 2:15 a white Lexus screeched to a halt in the parking lot. A flustered Malongo trotted in, breathless, followed by a driver carrying his clubs and golf shoes.

"Bloody traffic," Malongo muttered. "Did we lose our tee time?"

"Don't worry," grinned Harvi. "Anyone else might have been scratched but I think they'll cut the chief of police and the chairman of JGM a little slack."

Both men preferred to walk the course although they could have driven golf carts. Caddies were not obligatory, but each hired a caddy to carry his clubs, Africans in spotless white overalls. Harvi's caddy Adam was someone he knew well and whose advice he valued. He reckoned Adam knew the course so well that his advice was worth a stroke a hole.

The two players' golfing skills were roughly the same and after eight holes they were three apiece with two halved, so everything depended on the last hole. No money, but major bragging rights were at stake.

The ninth hole at Woodmead is a four hundred yard par four, slight dogleg left, the second toughest hole on the front half of the course. There is water on the right but not in the line of flight. Harvi and Malongo both hit adequate drives followed by mediocre fairway woods and then managed to chip onto the green. Malongo left his first putt short by four feet but sank his second for a bogey.

Harvi's first attempt rolled five feet past the hole, leaving him with a tricky downhill putt for bogey. He looked at his caddy.

"Just a tap. Aim six inches right," said Adam.

Malongo was looking tense, he loved to win. *Be very careful,* thought Harvi. He lined up, took a thoughtful practice swing and then hit the ball a foot wide. Hole and match to Malongo who beamed all over his face.

Adam frowned in disbelief.

"You were the better man," smiled Harvi, shaking Malongo's hand warmly. "By the way, I have a small favour to ask."

29

At noon next day my phone rang. It was Harvi.

"We have made some progress. The police have a line on the vehicle."

"That was quick."

"The commissioner and I have a good understanding."

"So what gives?"

"The police let us have the grey paint chips. We helicoptered them to the lab at our Kloopfontein mine. We have some highly skilled technicians there. They compared the sample with a database of vehicle paints belonging to Ford of South Africa."

"Why Ford, why not Toyota or Volkswagen?"

"We would have tried them all, but we got lucky the first time. You said it was a truck and there are a lot of Ford trucks around."

"What was the lab's conclusion?"

"We're looking for a late model Ford Ranger Raptor, grey, of course."

"That must narrow the search to several thousand. How does it get us any closer?"

"That was just the first step. We then fed that information back to the police. That gave them something they could work with."

"And?"

"They called the Department of Motor Vehicles. Turns out there are only sixteen such trucks registered in that part of Protea."

"That doesn't sound right. It's too small a number."

"This is a late model, remember. The paint formula was changed very recently. It's a special composition – super-gloss. Your driver may be a bit of a dandy, someone who likes to appear 'hands-on' but doesn't want to get his hands – or his truck – dirty."

"You've done well," I said.

He laughed. "I may only be a simple mining engineer from Latvia but I try to give the right orders."

Not so simple, I thought. "How can I keep the pressure on the police?"

"I thought you might ask. I have a name for you: Ian Smith."

"And he is?"

"Not the last white prime minister of Rhodesia. He's a young man in the police. To be precise, he is in the Directorate for Priority Crime Investigation, known popularly as the Hawks. He is the liaison between the

Hawks and JGM and I have a lot of time for him. He'll work with you to find your friend."

"How can I meet him?"

"The Hawks are based in Pretoria, but he is in their Johannesburg office in Parktown. It's only a mile from your hotel."

I thanked Harvi warmly. "You really put yourself out."

He laughed. "Carlton has done me a few favours so this is a chance to balance the books. Call if you need me."

∼

Encouraged by the conversation with Harvi, I called Carlton to thank him for the introduction.

"You're welcome," he said. "Is there anything else I can do to help?"

"I could use more manpower," I said. "Harvi was great but something in the way of helpers would be nice."

"What if I send you Halfshaft?"

Ron Halfshaft is a young computer programmer with a lively brain who lives down at the beach in Los Angeles. He is also a card counter who drives to Las Vegas on weekends in his yellow 1967 Mustang and has eidetic memory, meaning that he remembers everything he sees and hears. The Vegas casinos haven't spotted him yet, if they ever do they will bar him from playing. We've used him before. He's a bit unmanageable, but as sharp as a knife.

"That might help."

~

After talking to Oliver, Carlton made another call. It was to Ron Halfshaft.

"There's work for you in South Africa."

The young Californian was writing computer code, which he did for a living. He was sitting in his Hermosa Beach apartment tapping a keyboard and watching the sun set in the Pacific. He liked to count the seconds from the instant the bottom of the glowing orange disc touched the horizon to the precise moment the top disappeared into the ocean. It took two minutes. It was always the same but he timed it every evening, just in case something changed.

"I have a lot of work here."

"I'll pay you double."

"Okay."

"Go to Johannesburg," said Tisch. "Talk to Steele. He's at the Sunnyside Park Hotel."

That was the entire conversation. It was a tossup who was the more naturally terse, Carlton or the much younger Ron, but despite the age gap they had a good understanding. Ron rang off and started to pack a bag.

~

He travelled light. Whether he was driving to Las Vegas for a weekend's blackjack or flying twelve thousand miles to South Africa, it made no difference. He packed a spare pair of jeans, underwear and tee shirt into a twenty dollar roll-on zip-up bag, added a laptop computer and an electronic gadget he thought might be useful and, in the late afternoon, caught an Uber cab to Los Angeles Airport.

He had planned his trip using an on-line travel website – nonstop from LAX to London, then nonstop from London to Johannesburg, travelling on British Airways all the way. Then he abandoned the travel website, phoned the airline direct and bought his ticket. He liked to keep things simple with as few intermediaries and changes of airline as possible. He bought an economy class ticket, then remembered Carlton was paying and upgraded to business class.

He watched several movies, ate indifferent food, drank a little wine and slept a lot. So he was fairly fresh when he turned up in mid-morning two days later in Johannesburg.

30

Acting on Rod Harvi's suggestion, I drove to the Hawks office, an inconspicuous four floor building opposite Parktown bus station and asked for Ian Smith.

The response was quick and respectful. I was shown into a small office on the second floor. A tall figure got up and came from behind his desk.

"Smith."

I am six foot tall but he towered over me by several inches, and a shock of fair hair made him seem even bigger. He looked about thirty. His tanned face was intelligent and humorous. The sleeves of his white shirt were rolled up and he had the muscular arms of a tennis player. He pumped my hand.

I started to explain why I was there, but he waved me off. "So we're looking for a truck? I have a few ideas about that."

"Did Rod Harvi fill you in?"

"Pretty much. What do you make of Sir Rod?"

"Nice guy. Older than I expected."

He laughed. "Don't be fooled by the grandfatherly manner. He is very smart – he beat a lot of top notch rivals for that job. He's an underground mining engineer from Latvia who came up the hard way, but he runs rings round the rest of the so-called elite in that company. He also has the energy of two normal men."

"He thinks a lot of you."

"As I said, a smart guy. Grab a chair and let's see what we have."

He turned his computer screen to face me. I saw a list of numbers and addresses.

"These are the license plates and the owners' addresses for sixteen trucks whose paint matched the samples from your friend's car. Sixteen places where we might find a damaged vehicle. We have some legwork to do."

He printed two copies of the list and handed one of them to me.

"Let's go! We'll take my car."

At first we struck out. We went to the address of the owner of the first truck, but the vehicle was nowhere to be seen and neither was he. We made a note and moved on.

The second vehicle was sitting in the driveway of a construction company at the registered address. We walked around the vehicle, inspecting the paintwork. It was unblemished. Smith surreptitiously ran a finger over the bodywork. It was bone dry – no question of recent repainting.

A man emerged from a nearby office and approached us. He was probably about to ask what the heck we were doing to his truck. We smiled and beat a quick retreat.

The third time was different. The grey truck standing outside an office on the edge of town and there was a gash along its glossy flank.

"That must be the one," whispered Smith as we drove by. He was about to stop the car, but I prevented him.

"Wait."

"But it's the truck!"

"I know. But what's the smart thing to do?"

Smith was excited. "Go in there."

I shook my head. "No. Drive straight on before we attract attention."

He did so. After a mile we turned and came back, pulling in to a spot where we could keep an eye on the vehicle.

"What's the plan?" he asked.

"We watch to see if someone comes out. Who's the registered owner?"

He consulted his list. "It's in the name of a business, BC Holdings. That is interesting but it doesn't tell us anything conclusive."

"No, it doesn't. But let's see who appears. We might learn something."

I could see Ian's mind working. It was probably a bit outside his comfort zone but he nodded in agreement.

We had only been waiting fifteen minutes when a surly looking character emerged from a shed near the office. He was white skinned but heavily tanned, and was wearing jeans and tee shirt. He climbed into the van and drove off.

We followed at a distance. We found ourselves on the road to Biko City and before long, not entirely to my surprise we arrived at the offices of my audit client, Bosu Construction.

The man got out and walked toward the main office.

"Why am I not astonished?" I muttered to Smith. "This is where we find out what the heck's going on."

We followed him into the building. The receptionist, taken aback by our sudden appearance, could not stop us from sweeping into what used to be the office of the late Dinesh Bosu.

Behind the desk sat Haresh Bosu, Dinesh's brother. The driver was standing talking to him. They looked startled as we bullied our way into the room.

"What is this?" Bosu growled.

"You may well ask," said Ian Smith. He turned to me. "Who are these characters?"

I realised that, thanks to the pace of the day's events, he did not know he was facing one of the Bosus.

"This is Haresh Bosu, part owner of Bosu Construction," I said. "As for him" – I gestured to the man in jeans – "perhaps Haresh will introduce us."

"This is one of my drivers," said the Indian curtly.

"Well he is driving the truck that slammed into our car last night, when my companion was kidnapped."

"Impossible!"

"It happened. She is the consultant who is investigating the link between Pelec and your family's consulting company, Axton."

Bosu shook his head in denial, then turned to Smith. "And who are you?"

Smith nodded. "A fair question. Ever heard of the Hawks?" He produced his badge.

Bosu looked at it and his scarred face became a mask of extreme wariness.

Smith turned to the driver. "Now, my man, what's your name?"

The man mumbled something under his breath.

"Speak up," snapped Smith. The genial manner he had shown toward me had vanished, replaced by something much more hard-edged.

"Du Toit."

"First name?"

"Hans."

"Well, Hans, where were you two nights ago at seven o'clock?"

A sneer spread over the man's face. "I was in Durban, man."

Bosu interrupted. "He's right. We needed some

special supplies and Hans went to fetch them. It's a four hour drive."

"In what vehicle?"

"A company eighteen wheeler."

"Is that right?" I asked Bosu. But I knew he would back up Hans, and he did.

"Where was the Ford truck all this time?" I asked.

Bosu shrugged. "Obviously somebody stole it and crashed it. That is why the side is damaged."

The story was flimsy but there wasn't much more we could do. Smith evidently judged that, with Bosu's lying, it could be difficult to refute.

He nodded at me and we turned to go. As we left I turned to Haresh. "We'll be back – count on it."

I don't know if that scared him, but it saved a little face.

As we were driving back to Joburg I told Smith, "Your being a Hawk seemed to scare the heck out of Bosu."

He grinned. "The real name of the department is the Directorate for Priority Crime Investigation, DPCI for short. South Africans like catchy names so we're known as the Hawks."

"What exactly are 'Priority Crimes?'"

"Political corruption, bribery, stuff like that."

"Who do you report to?"

"To the police."

"Okay."

He nodded. "The Hawks replaced an outfit with an equally colourful name, the Scorpions. The Scorpions were suspected of being used by politicians of one party to spread slander about politicians of the other, so they were disbanded."

I thought about that. "I'm confused," I said. "So the Hawks investigate political crimes and yet they report to the police. Doesn't that mean that they can investigate their own bosses? It seems a curious arrangement."

Smith looked embarrassed. "Yes, and some say the Hawks lack independence because of it."

"It does sound an imperfect system."

"It is. That's why I keep in touch with Rod Harvi. With JGM's financial strength and the Hawks' political weight, we have a partnership that is free to tackle issues in a way that is free of corruption."

"Are the police okay with this cosy relationship?"

"Apparently. Harvi has a good understanding with Malongo, the police commissioner."

"Do you mean a financial understanding? That seems unlike Harvi. He seems pretty straightforward."

Smith laughed. "Maybe so, but to do business in South Africa you have to be flexible."

"And is JGM flexible?"

"Very much so. In particular, they have a global perspective on money. That appeals strongly to some of our government officials."

"What do you mean?"

"Think foreign currency. The South African currency, the rand, has nosedived over the years. In 1994 there were three and a half rand to the dollar and now there are fourteen. Who knows which direction it will head in the future. So the idea of having a nest-egg of hard currency in a bank outside South Africa can be very appealing."

"But illegal?"

"Not if it is reported to the government. But then people know you have more money than you are supposed to have."

"No offense," I said, "but there seems to be a serious shortage of honest government in this part of the world."

"Tell me about it," he said with feeling. "Want some lunch?"

～

We sat on the wooden outdoor terrace of the Pound and Penny pub at the Sunnyside Hotel, in the shadow of the trees. I ordered a hamburger, washed down with a glass of chilled Cape Riesling.

"We seem to be losing momentum," I said.

He nodded. "We know the Bosus are involved."

"But how do we prove it?"

"Good question. Our main lead, involving the truck, has been blocked for now by Haresh alibi-ing his driver."

"It's still a Bosu truck," I said.

"Of course. Things look completely incriminating, no question."

"Let's not forget Shiv, the senior brother," I mused. "Haresh may be loud and conspicuous with his scar and so on, but it's Shiv who really runs the show."

Smith nodded. "We've got our eye on Shiv. Although Haresh, with his glass eye, is in some ways an easier candidate. He's the hard man, the enforcer. He also runs the casino which is a whole other story as regards corruption. It's very successful but I suspect there is some major tax evasion going on there. It's on our list, we just haven't got to work on it yet."

"Your list sounds pretty long."

He sighed. "It is."

31

W e were silent for a while. The setting was idyllic. Birds sang high up in the huge plane trees that shaded the Sunnyside's green lawns. But their innocent music somehow only served to emphasise the grim reality of Lucy Gray's death and Rebekka's disappearance. I had not met Lucy face to face so I didn't feel her death personally, but Rebekka's kidnapping was another matter.

"How can we put pressure on the Bosus?" Ian asked.

"That's happening already, if slowly. Rebekka said she had finished her report on Pelec. She was sharing her notes with her boss in Chicago. Even if she is taken out of the picture, which God forbid, they should tell a pretty damning story."

"What about the embezzlement at Bosu Construction? The thirty-five million that went missing?"

"That will become public too, but things move at a deliberate pace."

"Pity we can't just walk in and turn that business upside down." Ian laughed. "That's the trouble with being the good guys, you have to behave."

"Most of the time," I said.

A thought struck me. "I agree about the casino, by the way. There's something bent there."

"Do you know of anything specific?"

"No. But it's a murky industry. All that cash attracts crime. The term 'moral hazard' comes to mind."

"How can we get a closer look?" he asked.

"By going there and gambling?"

He shook his head. "You and me? Not a great idea. We're both known to Haresh Bosu now."

"We need some expert help," I said. "Someone who knows their way around a casino. Know anyone?"

Then I snapped my fingers. "Sen!"

"Okay I'll buy," he said. "Who or what is Sen?"

"Omar Sen is someone I knew at Oxford. He plays high-stakes poker for a living."

"So?"

"He's mainly based in the South of France, but I know he plays a lot here in Johannesburg with some wealthy mining tycoons. I haven't spoken to him lately but if he's here he might be willing to help us out."

"What's he like?"

"He's an upper-class Pakistani who has never had to work for a living. Arrogant, but a brilliant card player. He wins tournaments and makes a lot of money. He would be just the guy to sit at the tables at Joburg Casino and keep his eyes open."

"Give him a call."

Which I did.

"Omar?"

"Speaking."

"This is Oliver Steele."

"Oliver, for goodness sake." The voice was clipped but welcoming. "You sound nearby, where are you?"

"Having lunch at the Sunnyside. I have a proposition that might interest you."

"Details?"

"I want you to go to Joburg Casino and play poker."

"I prefer the Marco Polo. You get a better class of loser there."

"There's a reason, trust me. Can we meet?"

"Of course. I'm playing bridge at the Country Club this afternoon. Be there in half an hour."

~

The Country Club is the pinnacle of Johannesburg clubs. There are other social clubs in and around the city but if someone refers simply to 'the Country Club,' that's the one they mean. It is dignified, serene and exclusive. Your average cook or bottle-washer is unlikely to be a member.

After explaining ourselves to the inevitable security guard at the main gate, Smith and I waited in the lobby. The clubhouse exudes quiet discretion. It overlooks acres of perfectly watered lawns. There is croquet, cricket and an elegant rose garden.

Minutes later, in walked Omar Sen. He was as thin as a rake in a narrow waisted dark-grey suit, white shirt and red silk tie. His bony, quizzical face bore a half-smile behind tortoiseshell glasses. The smile broadened as he saw me.

"Upon my word, it's that Oxford rarity, an intelligent squash-player. How are you, Oliver?"

"Very well. How's the university's least athletic poker player?"

"Mustn't complain."

"You look prosperous."

A smirk. "As I say, I can't complain."

"As a result of playing poker?"

He shook his head. "That was at Oxford. After I went down, I discovered bridge and it has become my main source of income."

"Really? I thought the two games were very different. Isn't poker about people's behaviour whereas bridge involves facts, namely the distribution of a deck of cards?"

"To some extent. But in bridge, despite all the bidding conventions, the lie of the cards is never certain, so the risk is always there. Should I go for a slam and risk the penalty for falling short? When there's a six figure sum on the line, it can be nerve-wracking."

"Isn't poker where the big bucks are? I've watched those Las Vegas tournaments."

He laughed. "Poker gets more publicity but bridge attracts the real money, at least where I play – in private, with wealthy people. Ask me where I live now."

"Where do you live?"

"On a yacht."

"Do you sail?"

"No, it's a motor yacht. I won it playing bridge." He reached in his pocket and produced a photo of a sleek triple-deck vessel moored to a buoy. I recognised the skyline of Antibes in the background.

"I keep it on the Riviera mostly, there or in the marina at Karachi. At the moment it's in Bahrain."

"Very nice! Must represent the winnings from a heck of a lot of bridge games."

He shook his head. "Actually, just one. We were playing on the yacht of ————." He mentioned a Russian oligarch, the owner of a British soccer club. "He bet his yacht on a single rubber."

"Was he drunk?"

"We both were. He looked a bit shaken by the loss, but he took it well. It was only his second best yacht."

"If that's your home, where does the oligarch live now?"

"On his other yacht."

"Is it as big as yours?"

"Much bigger."

There was a pause. We chatted about mutual friends for a while.

Finally, he looked at his watch. "I'm playing soon. What's all this about Joburg Casino?"

"Here's the situation."

～

Around noon the next day, Sen went to the Casino. He was new there, so nobody recognised him. He joined a table of half a dozen players, nodded politely and sat down.

He spent a few minutes playing himself in. He soon saw that he could trounce his opposition easily, but he took care not to play for high stakes and broke roughly even.

After a while he started looking around. He tried not to be obvious about it. Making an excuse, behaving like a player disappointed by his lack of success, he got up and strolled around the gaming floor.

The place was busy, even in early afternoon which is typically a quiet time of day, so he guessed the casino must be very profitable. In the evening, when things got really active, hundreds of thousands of dollars probably changed hands.

A dozen blackjack tables and four roulette tables were in use.

Omar considered roulette a mug's game with poor odds, but he paused to watch.

He was about to go back and play more poker when he noticed something unusual about the roulette wheel he was watching. The ball had landed on even six times in a row.

That sometimes happened, of course. There were only a couple of players at the table, neither wagering big money, so no great drama but it made him pause to see how it fell the seventh time.

32

Omar sensed something was off. The fact that there were only two players was not unusual. But as he watched, he realised that the dealer and one of the players, a young Sikh in a turban, knew one another. The dealer would spin the wheel, wait for the tiny ball to settle, then grin at the player, who sometimes won and sometimes lost. It was as if the dealer was showing off.

Not many people would have noticed anything unusual, but this was Omar's home turf and he knew a rigged game when he saw one. It was a certain feeling, something about the lack of spontaneity in people's behaviour.

He returned to his poker table and spent an hour trading chips with the other players – a burly young Afrikaner with more money than skill, a dark skinned middle-aged business type in suit and tie, and a couple of men in sport shirts who looked and sounded like British tourists.

A little later he got up and strolled past the roulette table again. The previous players were gone, replaced by others, but the dealer was still there. His manner this time was businesslike and normal. Omar saw nothing in the few minutes he watched to suggest anything untoward.

He went to one of the casino's bars and phoned Oliver.

"How is it going?" asked Oliver.

"You may be onto something," said Omar.

"Tell me."

"One of the roulette wheels is fixed."

"You're kidding."

"Nope. The Bosus may be using it to pay people off. The question is, who?"

"Who did you see winning?"

"Some young guy, and not consistently. I think they were just fooling with it."

I thought for a moment. "I hate to ask, but would you be willing to go back again, keep an eye out in case something happens?"

Omar laughed. "Okay – for a while anyway. I'm intrigued."

"You can use the time to win some decent money at the poker table."

"Actually, I can't. I could clean those people out in half an hour, but it would not be a good idea. I would be recognised and probably disapproved of."

"Disapproved of? A celebrity like you?"

"It sounds absurd, but it could happen," said Omar, unaware of the sarcasm.

∾

Ron Halfshaft, only mildly jetlagged after the long airplane journey from Los Angeles, presented himself to Oliver Steele at the Sunnyside Hotel.

"Hi," said Oliver.

"What's the story?" asked Ron.

Oliver explained.

"Where do I fit in?"

"I'm not sure. Carlton volunteered your services, so I said yes. Something will come up."

"Okay."

Oliver looked at his watch and then, on a whim, called Omar Sen.

"You free for lunch?"

"Maybe. What's up?"

"Got a fellow poker player here."

"Does he play bridge?"

Oliver looked at Ron who shook his head.

"I don't think so."

"Pity. I'll come round anyway."

∾

It was sunny, so they met outside on the terrace of the Pound and Penny.

Ron and Omar shook hands. They took stock of each other. Omar, even off duty, was immaculate in a narrow-waisted tweed jacket, twill shirt and flowered silk ascot. He was carrying a green Harrods carrier bag. Ron was wearing, formally for him, a clean tee shirt.

"Omar Sen? Didn't you win the CPPT Deep Stack Championship at The Venetian six years ago?"

"Yes. You have a good memory."

"I tend to remember stuff."

"CPPT: translation?" asked Oliver.

Omar said, "Card Player Poker Tour. It's a series of tournaments. That was actually one of the last poker tournaments I played in."

"Are you retired?" asked Ron.

"I play bridge now. It seems to suit me better."

"Never tried it," said Ron. "Is it easy to learn?"

Omar laughed. "Funny you should ask. I brought you a book just in case." He took it out of the bag.

Ron looked at it. "'Learn Bridge in a Weekend.'"

"It's a good introduction. The foreword is by a friend of mine, Zia Mahmood. If you memorise it from cover to cover you'll get a good start."

Omar was joking but Ron did not smile. "I'll do that."

~

Next day, late in the afternoon, my phone rang. It was Omar.

"I'm here at the Casino as you asked. I think we may have hit the jackpot."

"Meaning?"

"A man came to play roulette. He sat at that wheel. He has been there less than an hour but I swear he just won a hundred thousand dollars."

"Who is he?"

"An African in a good suit. In his forties, quietly confident. He could be a civil servant or a politician, he has that well-fed look."

"Where are you now?"

"I'm in the bar."

"Can you keep tabs on him?"

"I'll try. He's still playing but he might quit at any time. I may need help. What are you doing right now?"

"Nothing as important as this."

"Get in your car and come round. Wait outside the casino, don't come in, I'll call you if he makes a move."

I collected Ian Smith from the Hawks office and together we drove to the casino car park and waited. Twenty minutes later a phone call came from Omar. He sounded excited. "He's moving."

"Okay. Follow him and tell me what car he gets into," I said.

"Will do."

Five minutes later:

"He just cashed in his chips. Not sure for how much but a lot of notes changed hands. Here he comes now. He's crossing the lobby. He's talking to the parking attendant."

We had positioned ourselves close to the front entrance. I saw a solidly built African in a dark suit emerge and wait, tapping his foot impatiently. *He looks like someone in authority*, I thought, *he has that air of entitlement.*

A streamlined sports car rolled into view and the man got in, tipping the attendant.

"An F type Jag," said Omar on the phone.

"Guess he's trying to be young again," I said. "We're on it."

33

We followed the Jaguar in my Toyota, a suitably undistinguished car for the task – not many people will notice a white Corolla following them.

The Jaguar driver liked to go fast. He headed north on Jan Smuts heading toward Sandton, but then stayed straight, leaving Sandton on the right. I could see the unfinished Leonardo tower in the distance, topped by a construction crane.

"Where do you think he's going?" I asked.

Ian shrugged. "We're in the suburbs, respectable country. He could be heading for Bryanston."

The Corolla didn't have much speed, but we managed to stay within a couple of hundred yards of the Jaguar. We passed a big hospital and a few minutes later the Jaguar slowed and turned into a private driveway. We drove on by.

"What next?" I asked. "We can't go in without revealing ourselves."

"That's okay," said Ian. "I know the location now. We'll get the Hawks people to find out who lives there."

I looked at my watch. "Are they still open?"

"There is always someone there."

He phoned and got a return call five minutes later. He listened intently, then stared at me.

"It gets curiouser," he said. "That's a substantial estate and it belongs to none other than Haresh Bosu."

"Bosu is Indian. That man is African."

"Very perceptive of you," said Ian.

"Damn," I said. "We should have got the license number of the Jaguar so that we could identify the driver. It was too far away for my eyes to read in this bad light, what about you?"

Ian shook his head. "Sorry. I'm overdue to get my contacts replaced."

I phoned Omar Sen.

"It's a faint hope, but did you by any chance spot the license number of the Jaguar?"

He laughed. "I'm surprised you didn't ask me that half an hour ago. It's FINPROT3."

"Well done."

"There's no charge."

"We'll use it to identify the owner."

"Do that by all means," said Sen. "But I can save you a little time. I made enquiries here. The driver, the gentleman playing blackjack, is Tom Maputo, Minister of Finance for Protea. FINPRO3, get it?"

"You're a star!"

"Yes I am," he smirked.

"And so modest. Why 3 by the way?"

"Sorry?"

"I'm saying, if Maputo owns FINPRO3, who owns FINPRO1 and FINPRO2?"

"He probably owns those too," said Sen. "He sounds like that kind of guy. Can I go home now?"

"With our thanks."

Ian and I looked at each other.

"What have we learned?" he asked.

"I'm not sure. Maputo is friendly with Haresh Bosu, but we already knew that. The question is, why is he visiting him now?"

"Who knows? A business discussion? He may want another loan to piss away at blackjack. Or maybe he just dropped in for a nightcap."

"This may involve Rebekka," I pointed out.

"I hadn't thought of that. If so, time is critical."

"It sure is. Can you get the Hawks to pay a visit to Bosu Towers and see what's going on?"

Ian made another call. Then, "Someone should be there in fifteen minutes."

After Oliver told Carlton Tisch about the $35 million transferred to TransOcean Bank, Carlton called Paul Coward and Coward agreed to go to Dubai and investigate. He wasted no time and flew from London to Dubai the next day.

On the plane he was waited on hand, foot and elbow by several flight attendants. For most people, Business class with unlimited food and drink and flat-folding seats is more than adequate, but not for Sir Paul. For him, first class was standard operating procedure. For a price roughly ten times the economy fare, he had a cabin to himself with a huge TV screen and loads of fancy give-aways. He made a mental note to charge his fare to the South African low cost housing project.

When it became clear that he preferred male to female attendants, a young steward called Cliff was assigned to pay him particular attention. All part of the service.

He undressed and slipped between linen sheets in the cosy bed with room to spare. He made liberal use of the free liquor – by the time he disembarked eleven hours later he had put away most of a bottle of Courvoisier. He was ushered, tottering, through the fast lane into a waiting limousine that wafted him in air-conditioned comfort to the Burj al Thani Hotel.

He liked to stay at the Burj al Thani because it was spectacular and, being unspectacular himself, he hoped the setting would impress people. His room was on the 54th floor.

He went straight to bed and slept for another six hours. When he awoke it was eight o'clock at night. He dug out his little black address book and called several phone numbers.

His first two calls reached answering machines. The recorded voices were seductively welcoming but he hung up without leaving a message.

His third call was answered by a human being who introduced himself as Aziz. They made an appointment to meet downstairs in the opulently expensive Crescent Restaurant in half an hour.

He tried hard to remain calm as a young man of Indian colouring in pink polo shirt and tight white jeans entered the restaurant lounge and swept toward his table.

After a couple of drinks to establish the mood they went upstairs to Coward's suite.

~

At the same time they were going up in the Burj al Thani's ornate express elevator, Basil Heinie, Shiv Bosu's South African accountant, received a text update from a confidential tracer service that he subscribed to, informing him of Coward's telephone calls. The last call, to Aziz, was the longest so Heinie phoned that number. His call went to voicemail since Aziz had muted his phone, being now busily engaged with Coward. Heinie disconnected without leaving a message. He would deal with Aziz later.

36

S hiv Bosu got to his Johannesburg office in Sandton at 8 am. His secretary had left a list of messages on his desk. Most were routine but one was from Basil Heinie.

That would need a reply. When Heinie phoned it usually meant he had something sensitive to discuss. He and Shiv were both wary of email. It left an electronic trace. If you had something nefarious to convey, as they often did, voice was the only safe way.

He called Heinie. "What is it?"

"It's about the situation in Guinea-Malia."

"Yes?"

I've been following the newspapers there. They don't like our proposed deal with the copper company."

Shiv cursed. The plan was to supply data processing terminals to the state-owned copper industry. It was Heinie's idea and, Shiv had to admit, a good one. Quite apart from the sale of the terminals, it would entrench

Bosu deep in the entrails of the business, providing scope for continued control and the ability to extract cash from the business almost at will.

"They know almost nothing about it. What don't they like?"

"The fact that the Bosu group is under investigation down south. News travels fast in Africa. We're getting a bad name."

"What can we do about that?"

"Downplay the connection with South Africa. From now on, all communication with Guinea-Malia should be conducted through me. I will handle everything from Dubai."

"Okay," said Shiv slowly. Something sounded fishy. Empire-building by Heinie perhaps? Well, he could live with that. Lackeys like Heinie did stuff, you made allowances.

"What else is going on?"

"Paul Coward, the investor in the housing project, is in Dubai."

"Are you sure?"

"Of course I'm sure. Dubai is a small place. Word gets around. But I don't understand what he's doing there."

"I think I know," said Shiv. "When Oliver Steele was at Bosu Construction he overheard Dinesh talking about TransOcean Bank. Then he visited the houses at Kloofdorp. He met Basson and probably found out about the architects' fees wired to TransOcean. It was a big mistake. Dinesh and Van Biljon both screwed up badly."

"I will deal with Coward in Dubai," said Heinie.

Shiv was silent for a moment. Then, "Make sure the villa is completely secure," he said. "All our records are there. It would be disastrous if Steele's people got hold of them."

"I realise that," said Heinie. "We can handle it."

"I hope so. Maybe we should bring in reinforcements."

"That is not necessary," said Heinie. "But if you insist."

"I do."

Shiv ended the call and looked at his watch. Time was getting short. He was more convinced than ever that he should leave South Africa before the authorities closed in on him.

I n the truck carrying the kidnapped Rebekka, she struggled to recover her wits. She glanced at the man beside her. He was a dim figure in the darkness, big and heavy, his face lit sporadically by the headlights of passing traffic. She considered speaking to him but did not.

Who was he? Why had she been taken? The truck was clean inside, with leather seats that looked new – she thought she could even detect a trace of new car smell. That was unexpected, and not consistent with a common mugging.

A thought clicked into place. In her hotel room at the Hyatt Regency in Rosebank was a printout of her report on the project at Pelec. She had taken it back for some last minute polishing before she showed a copy to her boss in Chicago, and she had not yet sent it to him. She had made a few pencil changes but not many, it was essentially complete. Her strongest criticism had been of

Protea's Finance Minister, Tom Maputo. Everything pointed to him being either bribed or blackmailed by the Bosus on a large scale – several hundred thousand dollars – and now she was being abducted. There had to be a connection.

The truck had been travelling for twenty minutes when it swung into a driveway, past a security barrier that rose to admit it and crunched to a halt on the gravel outside a handsome white house with stone pillars on either side of the door. She was hustled inside and upstairs by her guard without seeing anyone else, shoved into a bedroom and locked in without a word being uttered.

Her phone and her handbag had been taken from her but she still had her wristwatch. It was eleven pm.

She explored the room. It was well decorated and there was a bathroom leading off it. The bed was made up, with good quality sheets. It was a bit like her hotel room at the Hyatt except that there was no telephone.

She inventoried the room to try to find something that would help her escape but without success. The windows were sealed, ventilation being provided by a modern air-conditioning unit controlled by a panel on the wall with a touch-screen.

As she was searching, she looked in the medicine closet above the washbasin in the bathroom. She noticed something apparently left there by oversight. It was a small gold locket on a thin chain. The locket contained the photo of a young woman whom Rebekka did not recognise. Engraved on the back were the initials L.G.

It did not register at first but then she realised with a shock what the initials might stand for: Lucy Gray.

The thought was chilling. Lucy Gray was the auditor whose battered corpse had been found in the parking lot of a petrol station near her Ponte City apartment.

There was nothing Rebekka could do, nowhere she could go and nobody to call.

She eventually fell asleep, but it was the worst night she had spent in her life.

38

She woke early next morning. Her digital watch said six am.

She tried the bedroom door but it was still locked. She went to the window and looked out. The sun was rising over a smooth lawn and ornamental flowerbeds. Should she try to break the glass? There seemed little point. The panes were double glazed. They might crack under a firm blow, but even if she could smash one without attracting attention there was a twenty foot drop to the gravel drive below.

She washed her face and dressed in her only set of clothes, then waited, frustrated. She was completely unable to communicate with the outside world.

After half an hour the door opened and a maid brought breakfast on a tray. There was bacon and scrambled eggs on a china plate, and a silver pot of coffee. There was also a glass of orange juice and a china cup and saucer for the coffee. And, surprisingly, plastic cutlery worthy of a fast food outlet. She assumed the lack of real cutlery was a safety precaution.

The food was welcome. She had not eaten for twelve hours and she ate swiftly. The phrase about the condemned man eating a hearty meal popped into her head.

She was trying to think of ways to get free when the door opened. In came two men, the leader with a swagger to his walk. The scarred cheek and the gleaming eye that gazed blankly over her shoulder were unmistakable. His companion a step behind was the big man from the truck, silent and obedient.

The leader scowled. "Get ready to leave."

"Leave where?"

"You'll find out."

"What's your name?" she asked although she knew that already.

"None of your business."

"Really? Are you so unimportant you don't have a name? Must I call you 'Hey you?'"

He blinked. "My name is Haresh. Get your belongings together."

"I don't have any belongings. Not even a toothbrush."

He shrugged. *He's not used to being argued with by a woman,* she thought. She sensed she was quicker-witted than he. Could she capitalise on that?

She began to feel slightly groggy. She stumbled and sat down on the bed. The ceiling lost focus and started to revolve. The room grew dark. She felt dizzy and could feel herself losing consciousness. She realised angrily that there had been something in the food she had just eaten.

Her last picture was of Haresh watching, amused, as she collapsed on the bed.

~

When she awoke she was in the back seat of a van. The van was moving, too fast it seemed to her, maybe eighty miles an hour. The driver was the same white man, probably 250 pounds in a stained grey tee shirt. He was speaking Afrikaans to Haresh who was in the front passenger seat. On the floor between his legs Haresh was balancing a gallon-sized glass jar with an orange juice label. The contents were brownish in colour but Rebekka could not tell what they were, possibly coffee.

Her wrists were fastened in front of her stomach with yellow garbage bag ties.

"Where am I?" she muttered.

"In a van," said Haresh. It was his only sign of humour.

"Where is the van?"

"We are on the way to Kruger Game Park."

"That's three hundred miles from Joburg."

"I see you know your geography."

"How long have I been unconscious?"

"About ten hours."

She looked out of the window. They were driving

through open country but clumps of trees at intervals cast lengthening shadows and it was clear that it was evening.

"Why are we going there?"

"You don't need to know."

"Set me down immediately."

He laughed shortly. "Be careful what you wish for. We are in the middle of nowhere and it's very hot outside. My advice is to relax. You are going on a game-spotting trip for a couple of days."

"Why, for God's sake?"

"She talks too much, man," the driver muttered. "Make her shut up."

But Haresh just said, "Things are happening."

"What sort of things?"

"It's business. You wouldn't understand."

If one thing really annoyed Rebekka, who was an accountant with an MBA, it was the suggestion that she wouldn't understand something because it involved 'business.' Especially coming from someone with, she suspected, less education than herself.

"Let me get this straight. We are going to wander around in the bush for two days. Why?"

Haresh hesitated. Then said, "It's a matter of timing. My brother and I are leaving South Africa and taking our money with us. That's easier said than done, we have to liquidate assets, transfer funds and so on. It takes several days. The releasing of your report at this sensitive moment would be a major embarrassment."

She listened with mixed feelings. The information

was crucial to her work, so her brain was churning as she pieced together the puzzle.

Then another thought. What if he did not care what he said because he did not plan to release her – ever?

39

The Corolla containing me and Ian Smith was parked by the side of the road in Bryanston, some twelve miles north of downtown Johannesburg. Ian's phone rang and he put it on loudspeaker.

"This is the Bryanston police, sir."

"Yes?"

"We called at the mansion. It belongs to Haresh Bosu, an Indian gentleman."

Ian couldn't conceal his impatience. "We know that."

"We did not speak to the owner, he is absent. But also at the house was Mr. Tom Maputo, the Finance Minister of Protea. He was just leaving as we arrived. There were also several servants, who we questioned."

"Yes?"

"It seems Mr. Bosu and a female guest are driving to Kruger Game Reserve for the weekend. They left a few hours ago."

"What action are you taking?"

"There's not much we can do right now. I know you wanted us to question the owner but we can't, since he's not there. We can go back again in a few days, I guess." The voice was mildly reproachful.

"Thanks, you've been most helpful," said Ian curtly. He ended the call and looked at me. "What do you make of that?"

"The guest has to be Rebekka. Kruger is a long way from Joburg," I said. "And it's a huge park. They could be anywhere."

Ian nodded. "As the man said, we may have to wait until they come back."

I shook my head. "I don't like it. Haresh is a violent man. Whatever he's planning is bad. We need to get Rebekka out of his hands."

40

Kruger covers an enormous area, more than 7,000 square miles," said Ian. "We'll never find them there."

"You don't think so?" I phoned Ron Halfshaft. "Where are you?"

"Playing bridge with my buddy Omar."

That was something new. "How's it going?"

"Okay, I think. But you'll have to ask him."

"Never mind that for now, this is more important." I explained the situation with Bosu and Rebekka. "Is there any way we can locate them by using their telephones?"

"Do you have their phone numbers?"

"I have hers."

"They may have taken her phone away from her. What about his?"

I cursed in frustration. "I have no idea."

"What's his full name and occupation?"

"Haresh Bosu. He's a director of various companies

but I doubt if that will help. He probably keeps his number private."

"Tell me the names of the companies."

I recited several of them. "But what can you do?"

"Have you heard of the Dark Web?"

"Is it something to do with the internet?"

"Yeah. I'll get back to you."

"Soon, please."

"Soon as I can."

~

I waited impatiently for half an hour before Ron rang back. I put him on loudspeaker.

"Write this down. His mobile number is 407 782 7228."

"Are you sure?"

"How many Bosus do you know who live in Bryanston and, at this precise moment, are half an hour's drive from the Southwest entrance to Kruger Game Park?"

Ian interrupted. "Inside or outside the park?"

"Inside. He's moving north-east at twenty miles an hour. Probably talking to the lions."

"That's amazing. How did you do that?"

"There are websites where you can buy the profile of just about anybody – including their phone number – for a fee. I put it on my Mastercard."

"How did you locate Bosu, once you had his number?"

Ron made a dismissive sound. "It's old technology."

"We need to catch up with him. Does that require some kind of electronic device?"

"Yes, I have it here. I could lend it to you, but it's a bit tricky to use."

"What do you suggest?"

"How about if I track him from here and phone you an update every few minutes."

"That's too unwieldy. You need to be in the car with us."

"Must I? I'm having fun. Bridge is super interesting."

I tried to sound patient. "There are lives at stake, Ron."

"Uh, okay."

"I'll pick you up in half an hour. Bring your gadget with you. Let me speak to Omar."

Omar came on. "You're stealing my bridge partner?"

"Sorry about that."

"That's all right, I understand the urgency."

"How is his bridge game?"

Omar paused. "I'll tell you later."

"Where are you both?"

"At the Country Club."

"We'll be there shortly."

~

Ian looked at me. "So, do we hit the road now?"

"Right. Just one thing: is there a four wheel drive vehicle somewhere that we can use?"

He nodded. "We would need to pass by the police garage to pick it up."

"It might be prudent, given where we're going – most of the roads in the park are okay but we could get involved in some off-road travel."

"Let's see what we can find."

~

We arrived at the Country Club in a fawn Subaru Outback – plain and not looking like a police vehicle.

Ron and Omar walked out across the tree-shaded car park to the security gate to meet us. While Ron was climbing into the Subaru, Omar took me aside.

"You asked about Ron's skill as a bridge player."

"Yes?"

"He says he's new to the game. Is that true?"

"If he says so. Ron never lies, he doesn't understand the concept."

"His memory is perfect. I've never seen anything like it."

"Yes, it's called eidetic memory, he remembers everything."

"It's a big help in bridge."

"I can imagine. I suppose he knows which cards have been played, even toward the end of a hand?"

"Yes, but it goes further. Bridge involves sharing bidding conventions with your partner and knowing which to use in any situation. It takes most people a while to learn but he seems to know everything already."

"Did you explain them to him?"

"Once, briefly."

"That's all he needs. Once he hears a fact, it's there in his mind. That would include conventions and how to use them. Does that mean he is an instant champion?"

"No. He still plays like a machine. But he and I are complementary. We would make a good team. I know the intangibles, which he has no feeling for – establishing table presence, how to get the best from your partner, We could make good money together."

"Ron's not interested in money. He lives in two rooms down at the beach and buys his clothes at J.C. Penney. His idea of a gourmet meal is chicken tacos."

"Still, when this is over, I'd like him to come and spend some time on the circuit." Omar shot his white linen cuffs. "He would need better kit, of course. The Country Club almost wouldn't let him in. He arrived wearing a tee shirt and we had to find him some proper clothes before they would let him into the lounge."

I laughed. "If he really has a future as a bridge player I'm happy for him. But right now, he's got to help us find the most dangerous criminal in South Africa."

41

Haresh Bosu entered Kruger Park via the Crocodile River entrance and drove about ten miles north, as far as the Malaborwa lodge.

Rebekka was still weak from the drugs. Haresh left her in the van, wrists tied, while he went to register.

"My wife is in the van, she's very tired," he explained to the clerk in the check-in tent.

Reaching the large canvas-sided structure he manhandled her inside. There were four utilitarian-looking bunks and he deposited her on one of them.

"Why are we here?" she asked drowsily. She tested her bonds but could not loosen them.

Frowning, he watched her struggle. Ignoring the question, he fetched the gallon jar of reddish brown liquid that he had packed in his baggage before leaving Bryanston.

"It's time to go for a stroll," he said. "We'll head for the perimeter."

She looked out of the tent's window which was made of some kind of flexible plastic. It was now completely dark. Bosu took the glass jar with him and ushered her outside.

As they stood in the open air, the layer of cloud obscuring the moon moved aside and visibility improved.

She saw with apprehension the outline of a beast moving in the bushes, fifty yards away. It was either a lion or something of similar size. As she watched, it emerged from the undergrowth and took a few steps towards them.

It was a lion, female and fully grown. From the lithe way it walked, it was in its prime. Its eyes seemed to be fixed unwaveringly on them, reflecting the moonlight.

Bosu took a knife from his belt and snipped away the ties round her wrists. He pulled her roughly toward him and unscrewed the lid of the jar. A fetid smell stung Rebekka's nostrils as he upended its contents over her shoulders. His purpose suddenly became clear, as she realised what he was doing.

Standing shakily in the dark, she brushed frantically at the sticky pig's blood on her clothing. She reeled sideways and almost fell.

Bosu turned and, breaking into a trot, covered the dusty ground from the perimeter to his tent. He reached the canvas structure and disappeared inside, leaving her alone.

The padding sound, barely audible, came closer.

She knew that wild animals in the camps were

normally not a problem. Despite their fearsome reputation, dangerous creatures such as lions and rhinos were much more interested in their natural prey than in human beings. The incidence of attacks on humans, even in un-fenced camps, was virtually nil.

But statistics meant nothing, given the rank odour of blood that assailed her nostrils. The watching animal was now less than thirty feet away, although still on the far side of the five foot high wire fence.

Don't run. Stay calm. With an effort of will she started to walk steadily toward the tent. But the arithmetic was not in her favour. The lion was getting closer with each step she took.

42

O ur drive to Kruger took five hours. We stopped once, at Ian Smith's suggestion, at a Spar convenience store-cum-petrol station.

"You should have a full tank when you enter the Park," he grinned. "It's not cool to run dry in the middle of nowhere with an angry rhino nudging your bumper."

He disappeared into the shop and came back with a paper bag.

"What's that?" asked Ron.

Ian showed him the contents, leathery strips of fibrous brown material with a savoury scent. "Want some?"

"That depends. What is it?" Ron was cautious in his choice of food, particularly outside the United States.

"It's biltong – dried beef. You can also get biltong made from game including kudu, which some people say tastes even better, but this is pretty good."

"Do you eat it?"

"Or chew it. Then when you've chewed all the flavour you can spit it out."

Ron looked unconvinced. "Maybe later."

"Please yourself." Ian bit off a slice and gnawed it appreciatively.

~

It was dusk when we approached the park. The orange sun was on the point of setting, its great disc tinting the clouds pink, and it was almost dark as we paid the 350 rand entry fee – about $25 – and passed through the Crocodile River Gate into Kruger Park.

Ron took the signal finder from his briefcase and balanced it on his knee. It was a metal device the size of a cigar box with an eight inch screen. I made sure the power cord was plugged into the car's 12 volt outlet.

"Where are they now?"

He consulted the screen. "About ten miles from here and heading north."

Just then we drove through a community of hyperactive monkeys, grey in colour but with black faces. They swarmed all over the bonnet and one plucked at the radio aerial.

"Those are vervets, they're everywhere," said Ian. "Ignore them. And don't switch the windscreen wipers on. If you do, they'll rip them off."

"They're cute," said Ron. He took a piece of biltong, wound down his window a few inches and held out the dried meat in his fingers.

In a microsecond a large grey monkey grabbed it, scratching a long cut in the palm of his hand.

"Sonofabitch!" Ron wound up the window hastily.

Ian passed him a tissue. "I told you to ignore them. Try not to get blood on the upholstery."

"You would think they'd be grateful," Ron muttered.

"Understand something," said Ian. "This is the wild. Every animal you see could be another animal's dinner before nightfall and that includes you. From now on, keep the windows shut!"

As if to emphasise his advice a group of elephants loomed fifty yards ahead. There were half a dozen of them, a few feet off the left side of the dirt road. They eyed the Subaru gravely, their great heads swinging from side to side. It was hard to tell whether they were hostile or just curious, but their bulk dwarfed the vehicle. I slowed the Subaru to a crawl.

"Keep moving," said Ian. "They won't bother you if you stay on the road."

I accelerated gently. "There's a young one over there. Does that affect anything?"

"Yes, the mother will be wary. But they are used to cars. They know they have nothing to fear. Which is just as well, because any of those adults could tip us over with one nudge of its forehead. Then we'd really be in trouble."

We drove on. Several times we saw waves of deer bounding across the plain, leaping on spring heels over anything in their way.

"Springboks?" Ron asked.

"Impala," said Ian.

"Good to eat?"

"Not bad. A clean flavour, something like veal."

"Where's Bosu now?" I asked. Ron consulted the screen. "Still ten miles away. Still moving."

"He could be heading for Malaborwa Lodge," said Ian. "He has to stay somewhere for the night and that would be the nearest place. The next camp would mean driving another fifty miles."

"Track him until he stops. We'll get as close as we can," I said. "What are these camps like?"

"They vary. The expensive ones are very comfortable, almost like hotels, with ensuite bathrooms and five star cuisine. Others are just tents – substantial tents but it's still life under canvas."

"Those sound more fun."

"They certainly give you a feeling of life in the bush."

Ron was looking worried. "Er . . ."

"Yes?"

"Do the lodges have boundaries?"

"Boundaries?"

"I mean, what about wild animals? Can lions and tigers roam around in the grounds?"

"We don't have tigers in Africa. Try India."

Ron flushed. "You know what I mean."

"Most lodges have proper fencing but, in a few of the simpler camps, game can come inside."

"This may sound dumb, but what if I have to leave my tent? Say I need to fetch something from the car late at night?"

Ian shrugged. "What about it?"

"Suppose a couple of lions are prowling through the compound looking for dinner and they spot me strolling along?"

Ian shook his head. "It never happens."

"So you say." Ron's voice shook and I realised he was deadly serious.

Ian said, "Even if a lion did find its way inside the camp, such creatures are more interested in their normal prey than in a bunch of humans."

I sensed that Ian and Ron did not really appreciate each other. I interrupted. "That's enough debate. Ron, check your screen and give us a reading."

Ron looked down. "He's still moving. . . no, wait, he stopped."

"He's probably parking," I said. "He could be checking into a lodge now, he and Rebekka."

I turned to Ian. "Can you tell exactly where he is?"

Ian peered at the screen. "I'm pretty sure that's Malaborwa. I've stayed there before."

"You may be staying there again."

"Really?"

"If Bosu is there, it may not be a good idea for us to just strong-arm our way in. Better to check in like normal citizens, scope things out, then make our move."

"That sounds reasonable."

Ron asked, "Is this one of the camps with canvas tents and no real boundary fence?"

"Yes," said Ian. He sounded amused.

43

W e drove north with Ron still muttering about the danger of a camp open to wild beasts. I made him check Bosu's signal every two minutes. It remained at Malaborwa, although with small changes consistent with its owner moving about within the camp.

As we drew nearer the lodge, I said to Ian, "Why don't you call ahead and reserve a room – or a tent, or whatever the term is?"

"Do we need one?"

"I don't know. How is this going to work?"

"The confrontation?"

"Yes."

"I don't really know."

"Neither do I. But we should have a base there, rather than working out of the car. That way, we won't attract undue attention and we can make discreet enquiries."

"I'll call ahead. They may be fully booked."

"I understand, but try anyway."

He called. Then: "We're in luck, we got the last tent."

~

The young woman behind the desk smiled. She wore a khaki tunic and shorts, and a badge that said 'Sally.'

"How long will you be staying?"

"Probably just one night."

"That's fine. Many of our guests spend a single night and then drive on up north."

I said, "A colleague, Haresh Bosu, may be staying here."

"That's right, he is. Will you be meeting up with him?"

"That's the plan."

She produced a map of the camp, showing numbered tents. "Here's your place, it's quite far from this office but you can park just outside it."

"Which tent is Haresh in?"

"Here." She pointed. "Over by the perimeter, fifty yards from yours."

"What does the perimeter consist of?" asked Ron.

"There's a wire fence."

"Is it electrified?"

She shook her head. "There's no need."

"What about the animals?" he asked.

She smiled again. "You needn't worry. They are much more interested in what they normally eat than in interfering with humans."

"How can you be sure?"

She laughed. "I've worked in camps all my life. I've never heard of a fatality."

"There's a first time for everything."

She looked at Ron as if he was slightly retarded, then turned to me and smiled. "There's no need to lock your car. Lions don't open doors."

We drove to our tent. There were lanterns at intervals. Their light was not bright – I suspected solar power – but it was enough to show where we were going. On the way I noted the location of Bosu's tent. We disembarked and went into our own.

It was more like a room than a tent, but with a canvas roof and sides and thick flexible windows. It was utilitarian but clean. There were four bunks, two wooden closets and not much else.

"What do we do now?" asked Ron. He still looked nervous.

"We wait," I said. "And keep an eye on the tent opposite."

~

Nothing happened for half an hour. Nobody entered or left Bosu's tent during that time. It was seven o'clock and pitch dark when Smith said, "Something's moving!"

44

From the corner of her eye Rebekka saw the lion vault the wire fence, clearly drawn to the scent of blood. She tried to maintain her calm, but she just couldn't. Her heart beat painfully in her chest. She broke into a run. She heard the animal's footfall drawing closer, padding across the dry earth. She got as far as Bosu's tent and grabbed the flap with blood-smeared hands, but it seemed to be tied from within.

She could literally feel the creature's breath on her neck. She imagined it sinking its teeth into her back.

She barely heard the gunshot that ended it all, such was the chaos of noise, stench and movement at that point. Reeling under the sensory overload, she passed out.

When she awoke she was lying on the sandy ground. Half on top of her, weighing her down, was the steaming carcass of the lion, blood trickling from its face.

~

Ian and Ron helped me as we struggled to lift the dead weight of the lion and release Rebekka from beneath it. Her body was shaking uncontrollably but she made an effort to appear calm. "Who do I have to thank for my life?"

"That would be me," I said cheerfully. Unlike some of my stiff-upper-lip compatriots I have no problem claiming credit when it is due.

~

Sally from the office arrived.

"I heard a shot. What on earth is happening?"

"See for yourself," said Ron.

She stared at the carcass and then at Rebekka.

"There is something strange going on here. Where did all that blood come from?"

Ron interrupted. "The lion, obviously."

"I don't think so." She touched the creature's face. "I see a wound between the eyes but it only bled slightly. Who fired the shot?"

I raised a hand.

"That was an amazingly accurate shot," she said.

"I thought so."

"An inch off and it would only have wounded the beast."

"Then what?" asked Ron.

"Then this young lady would be biltong."

"I'm an accountant, we're noted for our precision," I said.

Sally said, "She's pretty shaken, let's get her inside."

"Wait a minute," said Rebekka. She looked at me. "The fact that you are here means that you know what's going on."

"Yes, I do. By the way, this is Ian Smith of the Hawks."

"I have no idea what's happening," said Sally.

"That's understandable," I said. "To put it briefly, your camp is the scene of an attempted murder."

"That's incredible."

I nodded. "Almost so. But I think it's time to take a look behind this tent flap."

Sally tugged at the flap which seemed securely tied and raised her voice. "Let us in!"

Finally, the flap was pulled aside from within and a face appeared. It was Haresh Bosu.

"What do you want?" he asked.

As he took in the scene, his face contorted in apparent amazement. "Rebekka, my dear, what on earth happened?"

The surprise was clearly contrived. Ian pushed forward and flashed his badge.

"Haresh Bosu, we've met before."

Bosu scowled. "I demand to know what is going on."

"You just tried to kill this young lady."

"That's absurd. We are here as tourists. Rebekka is a visitor to South Africa and I agreed to show her the Game Park."

I'd had just about enough of Haresh Bosu. I brushed past him and went into the tent.

Inside, it was identical to our own with four simple bunks. Two were unused, the others littered with half-unpacked baggage. A frowning Abel was sitting on one of the bunks. He looked sullen and confused. An object on the dresser caught my attention.

"What's this?"

'This' was a glass jar with a screw-on lid and a label describing it as orange juice. It was almost empty but was smeared with the remains of a reddish-brown fluid that clung to the inside of the glass and clearly had nothing to do with fruit juice. I unscrewed the top and sniffed. The smell was sickening, like rotten meat and I almost gagged. I held the bottle up.

Sally wrinkled her nose. "It smells like blood."

Ian said, "It is. It's the same as the blood on Rebekka's blouse."

By now we had all reached the same grim conclusion.

Ian stepped forward. "Haresh Bosu, I arrest you for the attempted murder of this woman, Rebekka Moran. You do not need to say anything but if you do it may be used in evidence against you."

"This is completely absurd," said Bosu angrily. He elbowed past us and strode out of the tent.

He had to pause outside, because the occupants of the neighbouring tents were clustered around, eying the lion's carcass with amazement. I caught up with him easily.

45

He stood there, staring uncertainly at the knot of campers who had gathered to watch. He patted at his pockets.

"Looking for these?" I dangled his car keys. He snatched at them and I pulled them away. He made as if to head into the bushes, but hesitated.

"I know what you're thinking, " I said. "You want to run. I would too, in your shoes, but I don't recommend it. You're in the middle of one of the world's biggest game reserves."

He scowled, and I nodded. "We both know what that means. More lions. You might as well come back inside with us."

Ron appeared behind me. "We need handcuffs."

"We have duct tape," said Sally. She was getting into the spirit of things, now that she knew what was going on.

We secured Bosu, tying his wrists with double the

necessary amount of tape – not taking any chances. The lion's body was dragged away and put in a shed, to be buried later. Sally explained to the other campers that Bosu was a wanted criminal and that Ian Smith was a member of the Hawks. The twelve year old son of one camper asked for Ian's autograph and he gave it, looking embarrassed.

Finally, I looked at my watch. "What's for supper?"

"We have roast impala," said Sally.

"Those lovely creatures?" said Ron.

"Wait until you taste it, it's pretty good," said Ian.

~

In the tent later, Rebekka looked at me. "Remember what I said the first time we met?"

"About?"

"About not opening your heart to anyone?"

"Oh, that! I get that a lot."

"I want to apologise."

"Why? You were right."

"Yes, but you just saved my life."

"I'd have done the same for anyone."

She stared at me, expressionless. I think wheels were whirring behind her pretty, dust-stained brow. "So you don't have feelings for me?"

I turned away and walked in a circle. Fingered the tent flap, tied it with the ties provided, adjusted the ties so that both were of equal length. Finally, I said, "That's a tough one."

"What's so tough about it?" Some exasperation.

"It's just. . ."

"Just what?"

"Can we talk about something else?"

She gave up in disgust.

46

We drove back to Johannesburg next morning. At the Hawks office, Haresh Bosu was formally charged with the murder of Lucy Gray and the attempted murder of Rebekka.

I returned to my room at the Sunnyside and called Carlton to tell him the story. "That's two down," I said.

He grunted. "The trickiest one – Shiv – is still at liberty."

"At least now he doesn't have his hit man brother to help him."

"I've been making enquiries," said Carlton. "Shiv has a few other hard guys on his payroll, believe me."

"How come?"

"The Bosus are slumlords in a big way in Mumbai. They employ some pretty ruthless characters to collect money and intimidate tenants."

"But that's in India."

"I'm just saying."

"Okay," I said.

"Will Shiv Bosu be arrested?" Carlton asked.

"You're reading my mind. I'll check."

I called Ian Smith.

"Is there enough of a case against Shiv to arrest him?"

"I wish," said Ian. "He's damn clever, and white collar crimes are notoriously difficult to prove. Plus, he's still well connected with the government of Protea. My superiors will want to be very sure of their ground before they act."

I called Carlton back and told him what Ian said. He just grunted.

I thought things over and called Carlton again, half an hour later.

"I would really like to know what's going on in Shiv Bosu's head, and what his plans are," I said. "Maybe I should just go and talk to the guy."

"If he'll see you."

"I don't know why he wouldn't. He's probably curious to meet me."

"It's worth a try, I guess."

S hiv Bosu was in an angry mood as he sipped his morning coffee. He was reviewing his various business projects. Until recently most of them had looked pretty healthy, but now they all seemed to be heading downhill with increasing speed.

The housing project at Bosu Construction had stalled, thanks to meddling by Oliver Steele.

Then there was the situation with Rebekka Moran. Haresh was handling that. Shiv did not like his brother's sharp-elbowed style but at least when Haresh said "Leave it to me," you knew he would take care of things.

Now, another project was in trouble. It involved Bosu Voice, the Bosu family's in-house advertising agency. Shiv had succeeded in persuading the Protea govern-ment to award them its public relations business. He had put together a promotional campaign strongly criticising white farmers and landowners, making them, and also the white owners of the *Protea Times,* furious.

Had he gone too far?

By now he was increasingly resigned to the fact that it was time to quit, to cash in his chips, leave South Africa and retreat to a place of safety.

A place of safety? Yes, but where?

There were several options.

His homeland India, for one. It was a politically complex country, boasting 29 states – 36 if you included the Union Territories. Of its many languages, thirty were spoken by at least a million people. It offered considerable scope for concealing assets and income, and confusing the tax authorities.

Dubai too was interesting. It was small, but its financial sophistication and offshore status put it high on the list.

Then there was the United States. A big, wealthy country with a system of federal ID numbers designed to prevent tax evasion. But its once powerful Internal Revenue Service was now seriously understaffed. Yes, U.S.A. was a candidate.

Perhaps at the same time he would burnish his image by becoming a philanthropist, he thought whimsically. It would not be difficult – just a matter of making a few well-publicized donations.

He was weighing his options when the phone rang.

It was Sheldon Meyer, his Johannesburg attorney.

"Hi Shelley," said Shiv. "Good news, I hope?"

"Fasten your seat belt," said Shelley. "It's Haresh."

∾

An hour later, Shiv and Shelley arrived at the Johannes-burg Central Police Station on Commissioner Street to visit Haresh.

At the ten storey, blue panelled building, a stone-faced guard patted them down and they were shown into an interview room.

Haresh was sitting there. He seemed to have shrunk. He was as pale as could be, so that the scar on his cheek was barely visible. He wore an orange prison suit which clashed with his face.

"Keep things low key, especially in front of the police," Shiv had told Shelley. He knew the lawyer could be abrasive, it was a quality Shiv normally prized, but not today.

"Don't be too aggressive in front of the police, I don't want to make waves. We must not do or say anything that the authorities could seize on and magnify."

That's going to happen anyway, he was thinking privately. *But we must avoid the spotlight for as long as possible, while I make some financial arrangements.*

"Whatever you say," said Shelley. He found it hard to get excited about Haresh's detention, even for murder. He had been coming to this building for years, since back in the apartheid days when it was the John Vorster Police Station.

Many African protesters had been interrogated in its cells. There was Ahmed Timol, the teacher who plunged ten stories to his death after a week of interrogation and torture, or twenty year old Clayton Sithole who was found hanging in his cell just eleven days before Nelson Mandela was released from jail.

Shelley had even been present at the re-naming ceremony when Vorster's statue was carted away. So he could not get seriously excited about a run-of-the-mill crook, even when that crook was his own client.

"What the hell happened?" Shiv asked Haresh.

"Does it really matter?"

"Yes, it really does."

Bit by bit, Haresh told the story. When he came to the part about the jar of pig's blood Shiv threw up his hands.

49

Y ou are a damn fool," said Shiv, his voice shaking.

His brother scowled. "It was a good plan. It would have worked if Steele hadn't interfered."

Shiv shook his head. "No, it would not. The Moran girl would have been silenced, but the aftermath would have been a disaster. Think how badly it would look. She was investigating Bosu's ties to Protea. Then she dies in your presence. What are the odds? The story, and your face, would have been all over the media in no time."

"Maybe," said Haresh sullenly.

"Certainly. How did Steele track you down?"

"I have no idea."

"Probably through your mobile phone. They can do that. Where is the phone?"

"The police took it."

Shiv turned to Shelley. "What happens now?"

"He'll appear in court."

"When?"

"In a few days."

"Must I wait that long?" muttered Haresh.

"At least."

"And then I will get bail?"

"Assuming you are given the option. You may not be."

"That's absurd."

"It's a capital charge. You are a flight risk," said Shelley. "And your behaviour prior to arrest was problematic to say the least."

Shiv listened carefully. He was mentally reviewing his plans. True, he had promised to support his brother through thick and thin. But he recalled hearing that successful businessmen had the ability to turn on a dime, and he was turning now.

He smiled reassuringly at Haresh.

"Don't worry, we'll take good care of you."

Haresh did not look convinced. He stared at Shiv. "What is going to happen to me?"

There was a long pause.

"It's a complex situation," said Shelley.

"I might go to prison for years?"

"That's unlikely," said Shiv. He tried to sound reassuring. "We'll fight the case to our last breath. We have unlimited funds."

Privately he was thinking that the timing could not be worse. Investigators were closing in. His own arrest was possible. Shouldn't he get the hell out now, even if it meant abandoning his brother? In his mind the idea was becoming a certainty.

He was annoyed at Haresh for putting him in this position. His brother was reckless and this time he had gone too far. Self-preservation sometimes trumped blood ties, and such a time was now ominously near.

He stood up. "Come, Shelley, we have to see about getting Haresh the very best barrister."

He turned to his brother. "Don't worry, we'll see you right."

Their gazes met. As Haresh stared into Shiv's eyes he suspected he was being thrown to the wolves. He understood why, and deep down he did not resent it. If the positions were reversed he would have done the same thing.

50

I phoned Shiv Bosu.

"This is Oliver Steele."

Silence on the line.

"We should get together," I said. "You weren't at the *braai* so we didn't have a chance to talk."

"What do you want?"

"To help you."

"Why do I doubt that?"

I laughed. "Okay, not help exactly. But make it a bit easier for you to resolve your problems without going to jail for the rest of your life."

"We have no problems."

"Really? Your affairs are in a critical state. Haresh is in jail. Your embezzlement of $35 million of so-called architects' fees, and its movement from Bosu Construction to a Dubai bank will soon be public knowledge and will certainly lead to prosecution. Rebekka Moran's report on Pelec is imminent, detailing your bribery of

Tom Maputo. I'd say you are deep in the reeds on the edge of a very muddy waterhole."

A long pause. Then, "You may come and see me if you wish."

To say his manner was grudging would be an understatement. But it showed his willingness to grasp at straws, not surprising since, realistically, there was little he could say in mitigation that would carry much weight in a South African court.

Still, in law strange things happen. Hopeless cases end up with the accused wriggling off the hook.

How did I personally feel? I had no doubt that the last Bosu still at large was as guilty as hell. I considered it my duty to ensure that he paid for his guilt.

t this point, unknown to Oliver, his attempt to bring Shiv Bosu to justice was receiving an unexpected boost from one Princess Ranaraunaa, the daughter of the President of Guinea-Malia.

She was speaking to her father by telephone from Los Angeles.

"You have to say no to Basil Heinie, Dad," she said. "He's an absolute reptile."

"You're exaggerating, my dear," he said mildly.

She shook her head in exasperation. "There are some very mean people in the world, and Heinie is one of them."

Ranaraunaa, known to her friends as Rosie, stared out of the window across Venice Boardwalk to the yellow sand and the Pacific. The copper-rich African republic was thousands of miles away, sandwiched between Zambia and Zimbabwe, but it was very much on her mind.

No longer a student, having just passed her finals, she was now a newly minted PhD in economics from the University of Southern California. Her flat was pleasantly student-ish, a mess of textbooks, discarded gym socks and food wrappers from Subway and McDonalds. A squash racquet and a battered surfboard stood in the corner. But now, aged twenty-four, she was starting a new phase of her life where she had to think seriously about how to use her qualifications.

She could simply continue her reign as a society ornament and fashion icon, of course. It was a reign that had been going on since her undergraduate years at Cambridge where her wit and good looks made her an instant success at more parties than she could cram into her life. She seemed to excel at everything, both academic and social, even speaking at the Union, the university debating society.

The British newspapers loved the black princess. They pursued her relentlessly, highlighting her dress, her love life and her political future. It was with relief that she moved to Los Angeles two years ago and made a fresh start, concentrating on her studies.

Now, two years later, she was weighing job offers – a position with the World Bank, something at UNESCO – but deep down she felt she belonged in Africa. She wanted to help her country.

Her father, the President, was seventy and unwell. He was also, she thought sadly, naive. He had assumed office with absolute power following the death of his uncle in an airplane crash. But since then, being more democratic than his predecessor, he had delegated a lot of authority to advisors, most of whom Rosie saw as ambitious hustlers. She had tried to get her father to fire many of them, but without success.

The one who worried her most of all was Basil Heinie, the businessman from South Africa. There was something off about him, including a total lack of a sense of humour. His intense manner shouted at her to be careful. She had told her father repeatedly that he was not to be trusted. He was just one example. There were others and she was afraid that, without a firm hand at the top, a *coup d'état* was a real possibility.

But Heinie was the worst offender. She tried to warn her father but soon realised that she could only really influence him by being on the spot.

So after agonising for several days she found a tenant for her flat, sold her textbooks back to the University bookstore and bought a ticket on the long flight via Paris and Nairobi to Malia City, the capital of Guinea-Malia and her home.

52

In the presidential palace in Malia City, the
President's secretary coughed discreetly.

"Mr. Heinie is here."

President Sam sighed. "Show him in."

The President was not looking forward to this meeting. He was impressed with Basil Heinie, but his
daughter Rosie loathed the man, so he was faced with
upsetting either his advisor or his daughter.

He hated to upset people. That was not a good
feature in a head of state, but then he was only an accidental President. His uncle, the first President after independence, was killed soon after abolishing the absurd
British democratic system and replacing it with what
amounted to a one-party dictatorship. His control was
such that when he died his easygoing nephew Sam
inherited unlimited power.

But now, decades later, the world had changed.
There were stirrings of opposition – young activists who

criticised the depressed economy. Not that this was the President's fault. Copper was the country's only product. World demand for the metal seesawed in a broad range from $9,000 to $4,000 a ton and all he could do was stand and watch.

So when Heinie, a self-styled 'consultant' from Johannesburg approached him a few months ago, he listened.

Heinie had telephoned from the Malia Hyatt, the best hotel in Malia City. His pitch was simple. He would apply modern management to the copper mines and triple their profitability.

At first the President was not impressed. Heinie was an anxious looking man in his fifties with a fleshless face, thin lips and an intense manner. Strands of grey hair receded from his temples. His watery blue eyes did not stay fixed for long.

"What can you do for me?" asked President Sam.

"It's a matter of what I can do for Guinea-Malia."

The President was mildly offended. He understood the distinction Heinie was making between the country and himself, but he considered it rude for this foreigner to patronise him. He already had all the wealth he could ever use and, unlike many heads of state, had never leeched upon the nation he controlled.

"Go on."

"If you let me conduct a review you will see what I mean."

"What sort of review?"

"A study of the copper company's management."

"How much would that cost?" The President prided himself that he knew the value of a dollar.

"Nothing. My company would pay."

"What would it entail?"

"It would focus on reducing overhead. Besides that, we would analyse your sales and identify new markets."

"Well. . ." New markets sounded good. The President was wavering.

53

The Kenya Airways Embraer 190 carrying Princess Rosie landed at Malia Airport and a limousine drove her to the palace.

"Hi, Dad."

They embraced. Rosie's mother died when Rosie was six and the President never remarried. His daughter would sometimes tease him, suggesting that a consort would be appropriate, but he would just smile and say he hadn't met the right woman.

She soon broached the subject on her mind.

"What's happening with the copper company?"

"We're making a few changes."

"Changes?"

"In the interest of efficiency." Sam looked embarrassed.

"That's the first time I ever heard you worry about efficiency. Sounds like you've been firing folk."

He shrugged.

"We have to move with the times."

"Who did you let go?"

"A few people," he said vaguely. "Heinie handled it."

"That man!"

"I know what you think but he's smart. He's installing some amazing computers that just about think for themselves."

"Which he supplied at considerable expense?"

"Well, yes."

"What else is he going to sell to the company?"

The President shook his head. "Nothing. Apart from the new equipment, things will proceed the same as before. Heinie will play no part in running the business."

She shook her head. It sounded too good to be true.

54

I was in the lounge at the Sunnyside when my
phone rang.

"Hi, it's Rosie."

This was a surprise, but a pleasant one. I only know
one Rosie.

"It's been a while. How are you? Are you still in Los
Angeles?"

"No, I graduated. I'm back home."

Besides being a hereditary tribal princess and the
daughter of the President of Guinea-Malia, Rosie is a
college chum of my friend Kathy Smith. Last year she
helped Kathy and me to indict Fredy, the notorious Vice-
President of Kongolo whose Paris mansion was confis-
cated in a money-laundering scandal. Today Fredy is
behind bars, Kathy is home in Florida and Rosie. . . well,
apparently she was on the line.

"I'm in Johannesburg," I said. "I guess you knew
that."

"Yes, I got your number from Kathy. I need some advice."

"I'm flattered."

"You are busy sorting out the Bosu brothers and their State capture antics?"

"Something like that."

"Well their finance director, a man called Heinie, is trying to chisel into the copper industry here in Guinea-Malia."

"Chisel?"

"My dad the President has appointed him consultant to the copper mines."

"That's a terrible idea."

"Yes, well. The old man is a bit absent minded."

"Sorry to hear that."

"It's getting worse."

There was not much I could say. I had heard the rumours. The President was seventy, not old by First World standards, but Guinea-Malia was a country where people did not live to a great age.

"First question," I said.

"Yes?"

"Is there much cash in the copper company?"

"I'm not sure."

"Here's what I suggest," I said. "Find out what you can about the cash position and call me again."

"I'll talk to Herron, the managing director. He's a helpful guy. I'll get back to you."

55

For my appointment with Shiv Bosu, I drove my trusty Corolla to his office building in Sandton. It was less than a hundred yards from Rod Harvi's JGM headquarters, and similarly futuristic in appearance. His office on the tenth floor was vulgarly expensive with a lot of leather and chromium. There was the obligatory view of the Leonardo Tower. He shook my hand without enthusiasm. The trademark warm smile was notably absent.

"What do you want?"

"To give you some advice about your controversial business dealings in this country."

He frowned. "Which is?"

"Make a clean breast of things, a confession. Go to the municipal authorities in Biko City and, if necessary, to the Federal authorities in Pretoria. Say mea culpa, we bribed provincial ministers and embezzled hundreds of millions of dollars, we are sorry. Throw yourself on their mercy. Repay the money. You will go to prison, but you will get credit in the form of a reduced sentence."

This time he did smile, but without warmth.

"You are a very naive young man. Nothing we have done is illegal. Regarding the buildings at Bosu Construction, the agreement was clear. The architects' fees were high but they were perfectly legitimate."

"What about Pelec's coal contract?"

"A court would have to show that the company's actions were the result of payments that Maputo received. We shall say they were not, they were simply a matter of commercial prudence. And we shall prevail."

The trouble was, he might be right, I thought. He was certainly capable of arguing the case forcefully.

I suppose I *am* naive. But like other naive people I live in the real world. Lawyers on the other hand live in a world of lawyers and they sometimes reach lawyers' conclusions. I just hoped the real world was where Bosu would be judged.

Well, whatever would happen would happen. I had another angle to explore that I thought would cause him problems. I looked him straight in the eye.

"One more thing."

"Yes?"

"Do you know what your man Heinie is up to in Guinea-Malia?"

The chubby Indian stared back, his lips forming a smile that was probably designed to make me feel small. "Basil Heinie is my financial director. He's a very capable man. He is in Dubai."

"I think you'll find he's in Guinea-Malia just now."

He shook his head. "Not true."

"Would you be surprised to know that he has persuaded the President of Guinea-Malia to appoint him consultant to the national copper company?"

"That's nonsense. We have discussed Guinea-Malia casually but we have no operations there."

"You don't, but Heinie does. He is acting for himself there."

"Impossible."

"According to my sources, in a few days time he will extract a large amount of cash from the copper business."

"He would have told me."

"Are you sure?"

The smile became fixed. He was a professional cheater of other people, but I suspected the notion that he could himself be cheated was a bit too much for him. There was silence.

"There's obviously a misunderstanding," he finally said.

"Perhaps."

But I was satisfied. I had planted the seed of doubt, although Heinie was certainly smart enough to come up with a plausible lie if confronted.

And confront him Bosu surely would.

56

As soon as Oliver left the room, Shiv Bosu called Heinie on speed dial.

"You are in Guinea-Malia?"

"Yes, boss." The line was good and Bosu recognised Heinie's deferential whine.

"Why are you there? You told me you were going to Dubai."

"The plan changed. I am getting very close to the President. I was going to tell you. Good results should follow."

"When will that be?"

"Very soon. I've finalised the contract for computer equipment. It will make a lot of money for us, almost as much as we made in Protea."

Bosu let him finish. Then:

"I understand you are planning to transfer a major sum out of the copper company."

"Er . . ." Heinie was plainly surprised by Bosu's knowledge.

"And that you will deposit it in your own bank account."

"Where did you hear such a thing?"

"Is it true?"

"Of course not." The response was fluent, growing more confident as Heinie gathered his wits.

Bosu was pretty sure that the accountant was lying, but he backed off. "I'm glad to hear that. I knew the rumour was untrue, but I wanted to hear you say it."

"Sir, you know I am completely loyal. I would take an assegai in the heart for you."

"I know," said Bosu soothingly. "No need to worry. But I have a suggestion. I shall be flying to Dubai very shortly. Why don't we take some time at the villa to catch up on things?" He was referring to the mansion in Emirates Hills that was the headquarters of all Bosu's businesses.

"Of course, sir. Do you want to discuss anything special?"

"No," said Bosu. "We just need to take stock once in a while."

"I agree." The relief in Heinie's voice was palpable.

"That's settled then."

57

R ebekka and I were in the 1920 Portuguese Restaurant in Randburg, having prawns for dinner.

She had been there before and the manager greeted her with a smile. The dining room was not large and the atmosphere was warm and friendly with wooden tables and no tablecloths. A mural of a Portuguese country scene decorated one wall. Flags of Portugal and Brazil, bullfight posters and an advertisement from the France-Portugal semi final of the 2006 World Cup hung on the other walls.

"Have the prawns," she said. "That's why we're here."

They were large and came split open and grilled.

"Dip them in the piri-piri sauce. Watch out though, it contains ultra-hot chilies."

"Piri-piri?"

"It means 'pepper' in Ronga."

"Ronga?"

"A bantu language from Mozambique where the prawns come from."

She was right about the heat, but a bottle of Windhoek offset the chilies' scalding strength.

"What's next on your calendar?" I asked.

She grinned. "I shall continue what I was doing when I was so rudely interrupted by that lion."

"Your report?"

She nodded. "It is all but finished. It's very damning of the Bosus, of course. They committed state capture, entirely without shame and with a strong dash of racism."

"Racism?"

"As in encouraging anti-white prejudice. Specifically, against whites who own farmland in Protea, a favourite target of the provincial government."

"Who will read your report?"

"Tom Maputo will see a draft and be invited to comment. It is a necessary step."

"What's Maputo like personally?"

"A mixed bag. He's articulate and amusing, and supposedly has a bright future in government. But there are serious questions about his honesty. He's been seen at the casino a lot, and socialising with Shiv Bosu. That alone suggests funny business, Shiv being who he is."

"Bribery?"

"Yes."

"So you are exposing corruption, but the person who you are reporting to is corrupt himself. That sounds like a problem. Won't your report be suppressed, or at least distorted?"

"It's certainly an issue. Which is why I am protecting my backside by sending a copy to my boss in Chicago."

"Have you already done that?"

"Yep. I did it as soon as I got back from Kruger."

"Good thinking."

"His copy includes all the supporting detail – sources, e-mails and so on – enough to bury the Bosus as well as various Protea officials."

"So you will be in the news?"

She shook her head. "My firm discourages the cult of personality. They prefer an image of professionals working as a team. Which is more or less true."

"More or less?"

"Sometimes more, sometimes less."

58

When Shiv Bosu got to his office next morning, there was an angry email from Tom Maputo. He was excited by an article in that morning's *Protea Times* about Bosus' public relations company, *Bosu Voice*. The article mentioned Maputo unfavourably.

He and Shiv had an edgy relationship. Maputo was sociable, witty and academically brilliant – all talents conducive to political success. It was unfortunate about the gambling.

He first met the brothers at their casino. When Haresh learned what Maputo did for a living he granted him a generous line of credit, suspecting he would run straight through it. Sure enough, in three months Maputo owed the casino almost two hundred thousand dollars.

At that point, Shiv brought pressure to bear. The

Bosu group included a public relations division, Bosu Voice, whose function was to circulate favourable information about its customers, design pamphlets, arrange interviews and so on. Shiv proposed that Bosu Voice do something similar for Protea. The account, he hinted, should be worth a million dollars a year.

When Maputo showed reluctance, Shiv reminded him of the casino loan. Fearful of exposure, Maputo gave in meekly.

Bosu Voice set to work with a will. For a million a year they didn't mind putting in some time.

White ownership of land was an emotive issue in Protea, as elsewhere. Afrikaners owned most of the farmland. They had done so for generations, ever since their Dutch *Voortrekker* ancestors first ventured into the interior. With the coming of universal suffrage in 1994 there was a lot of talk of redistribution but not much actually happened.

Maputo did not really care about the land – he was no farmer – but the issue was an obvious vote-winner. So he did not discourage Bosu Voice from emphasising the subject, vilifying white landowners and calling for action.

The *Protea Times* understood what Bosu Voice was doing and were not amused. The newspaper was white-owned and its owners were very uneasy about land expropriation, pointing to the chaos that ensued in Zimbabwe when it happened there. A loaf of bread now cost ten million Zimbabwean dollars and it was cheaper to paper your living room in Harare with banknotes than with wallpaper. So the *Times* shone a bright light on the relationship between Bosu Voice and the provincial government, with relish.

Shiv scanned the article. Several sentences caught his eye:

We have been examining the awarding of a Protean government PR contract to Bosu Voice.

Our reporters found that the government recently instituted special rules for awarding contracts to outside agencies. These rules make it impossible to hire a contractor that does not have an office in Biko City. The only reason we could see for this rule, introduced shortly before giving the contract to Bosu Voice, was that it disqualified BV's competitors.

Another rule allows Finance Minister Thomas Maputo to singlehandedly award such business.

Mr. Maputo recently claimed about 100,000 rand for business expenses incurred at Casino Joburg, owned by the Bosus.

It is essential, in our opinion, that the municipal government's contract with Bosu Voice be voided. Bosu Voice should repay all fees received, which were excessive.

Shiv tore out the page, crumpled it into a ball and threw it in the wastepaper basket. The phone rang. It was Maputo.

"Shiv, my friend, you must help me."

"Really?"

"Did you get my email?"

"Sure, I've been reading the piece in the *Times*."

"It's dreadful."

"Typical muckraking journalism, I've seen worse. I thought it was pretty dull."

"This is the end for me!"

"Calm down."

"You don't understand. My career is based on a clean image. This report implies that I am corrupt."

"That's your problem, not mine," said Shiv. The words just slipped out.

There was a shocked silence from Maputo.

Then, "If that's your attitude I may have to release notes showing how you blackmailed me into awarding you that contract."

"That's called shooting yourself in the foot."

"If I go down, I shall take you with me."

"You can't prove I did anything wrong," snapped Shiv. "It's not my fault you are a hopeless gambler."

"You understand nothing." Maputo's voice shook as he slammed down the phone.

Not much goodwill left in that quarter, Shiv thought drily. But as he considered the implications, he saw that they were not good. He could feel the walls closing in. Any day now, prompted by the news reports, law enforcement would be asking questions. It reinforced his conviction that he must leave the country, and soon.

In his mind he made a list of the steps he must take:

One: transfer as much cash as possible out of South Africa.

Two: alert his attorney Shelley Meyer to prepare a

blizzard of motions opposing any legal action against him or his companies.

Three: alert the pilot of his private plane to be ready for a flight.

Missing from the list were any steps to help his brother Haresh.

59

S hiv called his pilot, Jake Smyth, and told him to be ready to leave in a few hours.

"No worries, mate," said Smyth. "Where are we going?" The former Qantas pilot liked to play the bluff Aussie, it seemed to inspire confidence.

"Do you need to know?"

"No, that's cool." He was paid a lot of money for not arguing with Shiv.

Next, Shiv turned to banking arrangements.

First, he added up how much cash his various businesses had in South African banks – it came to just over a hundred million dollars.

He then set about transferring the money into a number of personal accounts in his name that were scattered around the world. They were in banking centres including Panama, Cyprus, the Cayman Islands, and the tiny republic of Kiribati.

He was particularly fond of Kiribati because of its

unusual relationship with the International Date Line. The line runs due North-South for most of its length, but near Kiribati it curves round to the east by almost 2,000 miles, leaving Kiribati, which is an extended cluster of tiny islands, on its western side. The capital, Tarawa, is thus the first financial centre in the world where banks open for business each morning. Shiv reasoned that in a situation where time was critical it might help to have funds there one day.

Most tax havens offer secrecy and independence as standard. But Shiv never believed the official line about that – even ultra-conservative Switzerland released information about certain accounts when pressured by the United States. Shiv preferred to spread his cash around several countries. If one caved in and gave him away, he reasoned, he would still have the others.

So he took the hundred million dollars and divided it into several parts. Where there were limits on the amount he could send, he telephoned the head of the bank concerned and obtained clearance first. If questioned, he was brief: "I am rearranging my investments." At that level, between presidents, it was enough. Within half an hour, Bosu South Africa was stripped of its cash and those funds all left the country.

Including the new money, the total in Shiv's personal accounts was in excess of four hundred million dollars. With so many accounts and passwords he preferred not to rely on memory, so his last act was to update his banking information on a silver-plated thumb-drive that he kept on his keyring.

He looked at his watch. It was 11:30 am. On an impulse, he turned on the television.

The woman announcer was right on topic:

"An investigation into electricity supplier Pelec has raised some major questions. According to sources, industrialist Shiv Bosu bribed Protea's Minister of Finance to grant Bosu Coal a contract to supply Pelec. The minister is said to have frequented the Bosus' casino and incurred major gambling debts. These were used as leverage by Bosu Coal to win the contract."

A grainy black and white photo flashed on screen. With a shock Shiv saw it was himself.

He cursed out loud. First Bosu Construction, then Bosu Voice and now this. He opened his briefcase and shovelled papers in, noticing with dismay that his hand was shaking. He called downstairs to his driver and, minutes later, he was in the back of his Mercedes as it purred through Joburg traffic.

The car stopped first at his house, where his servant packed a bag while he waited downstairs in the velvet-papered living room. Then he set out again, this time for the airport.

60

Despite Rosie's protests, Basil Heinie was hired by the President of Guinea-Malia to assess the management of the copper business.

His first action was to interview the company's manager, Bill Herron.

Herron was a bland Englishman of medium height, with brown eyes and sandy hair. There was nothing special about his appearance but he had a knack for getting on well with people, and a golf handicap in single figures. He was in his fifties, popular in the community and held several civic positions including that of chairman of the local Rotary chapter.

Heinie walked into Herron's office, a plain room with a large metal desk and a couple of upright chairs for guests. On the desk were neat piles of papers and a framed photo of his wife and teenage children, a boy and a girl. Heinie sat down without shaking hands.

"I have been reviewing staffing levels and I am shocked by what I found."

"Really?"

Heinie nodded. "The accounting department is particularly large."

"That's true. There are reasons, though."

"I can't imagine what they are." Heinie jabbed a pencil in front of Herron's face. "There is a room full of clerks – ten people – who do nothing but summarise data and forward it to the person who maintains the general ledger."

Herron nodded. "The chief accountant, right."

"That person transfers the totals to the ledger once a month and produces a profit and loss account."

"Correct."

Heinie spread his hands wide. "Haven't you heard of computers, my friend?"

Herron was surprised at Heinie's directness but he did not take offense. He had experienced much worse. Before coming to Guinea-Malia he had worked in Robert Mugabe's Zimbabwe amid the chaos that led to the total destruction of the nation's currency. Since the hyperinflation, commerce there was conducted in American dollars. So he was used to just about anything.

He smiled. "I have a powerful desktop system at home and I use the internet all the time."

"Then surely you can see that the company should be computerised, which would save dozens of jobs?"

Herron nodded, his round face expressionless.

"New to Guinea-Malia, are you, Mr. Heinie?"

Heinie shrugged.

"I'll take that as a yes. Myself, I've been here twenty years. As you may know, there's a lot of unemployment here. And the level of education is low.

"I do know that," Heinie snapped.

Herron raised a hand.

"When I came here we set up a system: wherever a column of figures needed to be totalled it was totalled twice, by two separate clerks. Neither man – they were all men – was shown the other's work. If the totals agreed, fine. If not, the file was passed to a third clerk and a third total obtained. This would hopefully agree with one of the first two, in which case the amount was confirmed. If not, the process began all over again. In the end the work got done, however slowly."

"That's ridiculous."

"We use a similar system in Shipping and also out in the field when tonnage has to be measured. It may be inefficient, but it provides jobs for a lot of warm bodies."

"Why have you not updated the process?"

"In a way we have. We've given people calculators instead of making them add columns of numbers with a pencil. But we still use what we call the double buddy system."

"That's the dumbest thing I've ever heard."

Herron grinned. "It is pretty dumb. But it means nobody is ever made redundant."

Heinie shook his head in exasperation. "I shall talk to the President about this."

"Feel free. But be warned, his late father liked the idea too, and the President had great respect for the old man."

After Rosie talked to her father, she suspected he had not told her the full story about 'consultant' Basil Heinie. She also wanted more information for Oliver.

So she called Bill Herron.

Herron had lived in Guinea-Malia for many years and she trusted him. He was pleased to hear from her, but his voice sounded strained on the phone. She suggested lunch.

They met at the Royal Malia Golf Club. The 'Royal' in the name reflected the old colonial days. The country was technically a democracy now, although the ruling Congress Party, headed by the President, regularly garnered ninety percent of all votes cast.

The club was the centre of Malia social life. President Sam and his uncle the first President had both played – they were keen hackers for whom breaking a hundred was cause for celebration even though the first President cheated a lot.

The golf course itself was crude, being bulldozed out of dry sand. Not much could be done to improve it. Once a ball was off the fairway it was in the desert. But the clubhouse was well up to European standards, spacious and air conditioned.

Herron ordered a steak, imported from Zimbabwe. Rosie chose grilled freshwater crayfish, caught in the upper reaches of the Zambezi where it ran through Guinea-Malia on its way to Victoria Falls.

"What's happening at the company?" she asked as they attacked their food.

"I don't know."

"What do you mean? You're its head."

"Not any more. I was fired."

She dropped her fork in surprise. No wonder her father had looked embarrassed.

"Why?"

"I did not agree with Basil Heinie's plans for the company."

"What upset you in particular?"

"How much time do you have?"

"Give me the whole sordid truth," she said. "After five years studying law and economics, I can probably absorb it."

He grinned ruefully. "He is introducing systems based on software written for some Swiss accounting machinery."

"Is that bad?"

"On its face, no. But it does require that clerks feed correct information into it. Remember the old saying, 'Garbage in, garbage out?' People in Switzerland probably input accurate data. It's different here. Guinea-Malia doesn't exactly generate legions of top accounting talent."

"Meanwhile, you've been kicked out?"

"Yep. Heinie has moved into my office."

She whistled. "He plays hardball."

They ate in silence.

"What will you do with your life now?" Rosie asked.

He brightened. "Play more golf. Carol and the kids like it here so I think we'll stay. I'm a life member of the Club, not to mention a Guinea-Malian citizen."

"I'm going to do something about this," said Rosie.

He looked doubtful. "What can you do? The President is . . ." He hesitated.

She nodded. "You don't have to be tactful, I know he's getting past it. But I have some other ideas."

"There's one particular aspect of this that really disturbs me," said Herron.

"Yes?"

"The computers Heinie is installing."

"What about them?"

"They can be operated remotely via the internet."

"So?"

"So someone in London or New York or wherever could log in and change the accounting if they knew the password."

"Would they do that? How would anyone in those places even know?"

"It's just a thought," said Herron.

After lunch they walked through the gardens and along an avenue of palms to the car park where Herron's five year old Peugeot was waiting. He's a decent man, thought Rosie, nothing flashy about him.

"Does the company keep much money in the bank?" she asked.

"Normally, no. But there are times when the kitty is flush – for example, when a customer has just paid for a major shipment. Then there can be millions. It only stays there briefly. All funds are transferred to government-owned accounts the next day."

She nodded. "Just asking."

"I know what you're thinking," he said, "but it's probably not an issue."

"Probably?"

"That's what I said."

62

Rosie called me.

"Hi. You asked about cash in the mining company."

"Yes?"

"There's not much now, but at certain times there is a lot."

"Is one of those times soon?"

"I'm not sure. By the way, the managing director has been fired. Heinie has taken his place. He has installed computers with access to the company's bank accounts."

"Ouch!"

"So in theory the company's cash could be sucked out by some bad operator in London or New York."

"Or Dubai," I suggested.

"Dubai?"

"Bosu has an office in Dubai," I said. "Just a thought."

"Now I'm really nervous."

"When is the next inflow of cash?"

"I'll ask Herron."

～

She called later.

"A major transfer is expected next week. About twenty million dollars. It is payment for copper sold to the Peoples' Republic of China."

"I'd be seriously worried about that money," I said.

"What can we do?"

"Is there any way you can get Heinie removed?"

"Not a chance. Dad is very stubborn, it's a feature of his condition. He won't change his mind."

"Hmm. Leave it with me, I've got a few thoughts," I said.

But I was not as confident as I tried to sound. I was afraid Heinie's position was unassailable.

63

Another call from Carlton. There are times when I wish he would leave me alone, he invariably calls when I am tired and not in the mood to be cross examined by an abrasive New York financier thousands of miles away who thinks he knows all the answers. So I may have sounded terse.

"What's so urgent?"

"It's Paul Coward."

"Yes?"

"I sent him to Dubai to look into TransOcean Bank, as we discussed. Now he's missing."

"Missing?"

"Not to be found in his hotel room."

"Should I be concerned? I didn't take to him when we met in London."

"He's not everyone's cup of tea," said Carlton. "Gay as they come, of course."

"Is his disappearance related to that?"

"Possibly. Or it could involve South Africa."

"I don't know how I'd start to look into it," I said. "What we really need is a man on the ground in Dubai."

"Not me, if that's what you're thinking," said Carlton.

"Why not?"

"I'm busy."

"Busy sailing?"

"Anything wrong with that?"

"Not if it's your whole universe. But meanwhile, people in the real world are disappearing."

Carlton said nothing. Had I actually made him think?

"Do you have any business interests in Dubai?" I asked.

"A few. There's an investment fund run by some Swiss folk I haven't talked to lately. It's done well, earns ten percent a year."

"Only ten? That's not much by your standards."

"That's for the investors. I'm the promoter. I make more than the investors, that's the whole point."

For Carlton, investors were the great unwashed. They existed to make money for him, not for themselves.

"How do you make out yourself?"

"With management fees I double my investment every year."

I was silent for a moment. Then, "Swiss, eh? Do they ski?"

"Why do you ask?"

"You can ski in Dubai."

"Impossible. It's 80 degrees there, almost year-round."

"Nevertheless, there's an indoor slope with machine-made snow and live penguins. Grab your skis and head on over."

Carlton sniffed. "Seriously, what do you want me to do?"

"Find Coward. It does sound as though he's been abducted."

"And then?"

"Rescue him of course," I said. "Whoever was responsible for Lucy Gray's death and Rebekka's abduction probably kidnapped him."

"I'll think about that."

"You sound pretty casual."

But I knew he would apply his mind to it. You don't get to be a billionaire by being casual.

Carlton hadn't finished. "What's up with Shiv Bosu?"

"At this precise moment I have no idea. I'll have to check."

"Is he still in Johannesburg?"

"I said I'll have to check."

"If you would, please."

Pompous little man. But it was a fair question. I called Ian Smith.

"Is Shiv still in Joburg?"

"I'm not sure."

"We should see what is happening to his private jet," I said. "If it's not at the airport, then he's probably gone."

"Good point," said Ian. Fifteen minutes later, he telephoned. "You're right. He's left town."

"As I feared. He'll be on his way to Dubai, never to return, at least not willingly."

Ian swore under his breath. But after a moment he cheered up. "Well, the government can thank you for finally exposing these scoundrels, even if one of them escaped."

"For now," I said.

"What do you mean?"

"I have some ideas."

64

I called Omar. "Fancy a cup of tea?"
      "The Club in half an hour?"
      "Perfect."

~

"How's the bridge going?" I asked. We were settled in comfortable armchairs, teacups in hand, looking out across the Country Club's immaculate lawns. On the cricket pitch a white-clad bowler trotted up to the wicket and delivered a leg break. The ball bounced short and the white-clad batsman swept it past square leg to the boundary. The umpire signalled four runs.

"It's going well. Although I've almost exhausted the Joburg seam, to use a mining term."

"Meaning?"

"I make my money by winning."

"Aren't you winning anymore?"

"It's the other way around. I've been playing with a group of mine owners who have more money than God and I've won a lot of it. Trouble is, they are getting tired of losing."

"Aren't they good players?"

"They're very good. But I'm better."

I tried not to smile. Omar might play world class bridge but modesty was not his strong suit.

"So they're crying uncle?"

"That's about it."

"What will you do next?"

"I'll move on."

"Where to?"

He shrugged. "There are plenty of wealthy bridge players around the world – hedge fund managers in Manhattan, Internet moguls in California, shipping tycoons in Hong Kong. Someone will always give me a game." He laughed. "Which is just as well – it costs a million dollars a year to keep that yacht of mine going."

"That much?"

"Sure. Mooring fees, maintenance, salaries."

"How large is the crew?"

"Six people."

I nodded. "I have a suggestion. Shiv Bosu has left Johannesburg and I'm pretty sure he is heading for Dubai. If so, I must go there too."

"That makes sense."

"Did you say your yacht was in Bahrain?"

"Yep. The sheikh's nephew – who is also the minister of finance – plays a decent game."

"Okay. Since it's in the region already, why not move it to Dubai? Ron and I can stay on board. Also, if you are finished here, you can go there yourself. You and Ron can play bridge and win some money while I'm dealing with Shiv Bosu. Everyone will be happy."

He looked thoughtful. "It might work. Dubai's mooring fees are no worse than the south of France. And I can think of a couple of players who wouldn't mind a spot of high-stakes R and R in Dubai – there's a young social media whiz and a famous Egyptian actor. I'll give them a call."

"How long is the trip from Bahrain?"

"Six hundred miles. Two days journey."

"Do it."

"Okay."

65

C arlton Tisch was down at Soper's Hole on Tortola, the marina near his home, when he spoke to Oliver. His mind was half on South Africa but the other half on his yacht, Guinevere.

Guinevere had survived the two hurricanes that devastated Tortola – *Irma* and *Maria*. She was safely enclosed in a concrete and steel boathouse whose vertical I-beams descended twenty feet into solid rock. The roof was anchored with cast iron girders to defy the wind's efforts to rip it off and send it flying. Carlton endured a lot of teasing when he built the structure, but he just smiled and said, "The day will come." In 2017 the day came. Irma destroyed half the island. Maria shredded what was left. A year later, smashed yachts still littered Tortola's serene bays. Carlton incurred some ill will based on envy, but he spent a lot of time and money helping others to rebuild.

When Oliver summoned him to Dubai he researched

the journey and found the best options were to fly either on Air France via St. Maarten and Paris or else by American Airlines via San Juan, Miami and London. Either way would take twenty-four hours.

He booked via London, then went and told his wife.

Mimi Tisch was used to Carlton jetting around the world. But when he said he was going to rescue a kidnapped financier in Dubai she raised an eyebrow.

"Is that safe?"

"Sure."

"Why not take Kon with you?" Kon Feaver was Carlton's best friend, twenty years younger than he, a jack of all trades from Tel Aviv, former Israeli Air Force fighter pilot, ex-professional soccer player, recovering alcoholic and a good man to have around in a bar fight or, for that matter, any kind of fight.

Carlton frowned. "I can look after myself."

"Of course you can." She massaged his sixty year old back. "I just thought you might like company. Two heads are better than one."

"I'll think about it."

~

A few minutes later his phone rang. It was Kon Feaver.

"Funny you should ring, your name just came up," said Carlton.

"Yeah. Mimi called."

"That damn woman."

"Something about looking for a body in Dubai."

"Not a body, a banker. She seems to think I need a bodyguard."

"Is she right?"

"Who knows? Where are you?"

"In the Keys," said Feaver. He lived in a wooden cabin on Coquina Key, midway between Key West and Miami. By day he fished. By night he ran a ferry boat from Havana to Florida for Cuban refugees who wanted to make a new life in the United States.

"Are you available?"

"I guess so. I don't have a run scheduled. Things have gotten slower since the end of 'Wet foot, dry foot.'"

He was referring to the rule that any Cuban refugee who reached US shores had the right to remain. The Cuban government disliked the rule and President Obama suspended it as a goodwill gesture to the regime of Raoul Castro. President Trump had not renewed it, probably happy with a measure that would both limit immigration and also please Florida's Cuban population, the majority of whom voted Republican.

"Meet me at the Burj al Thani in Dubai," said Tisch. "I'll reserve a suite."

"Cool," said Kon. He was bored and welcomed the chance of some action.

~

Kon could have driven from Coquina to Miami but he chose instead to take his own plane, an amphibious de

Havilland Beaver that sat on floats in a hurricane-proof boathouse attached to his cabin.

Going by air only saved half an hour, but he loved to fly. He taxied northwards parallel to the shore, soared into the air and arrived an hour later at Opa-locka Executive Airport, ten miles north of Miami. Sam, an old associate, ran him down the road to Miami in his truck. He made the flight just in time.

People asked Kon why he cut things so fine. He would just grin and say he liked the adrenaline rush. He travelled with hand luggage only. His 'Global Entry' card fast-tracked him through Security and he walked onto the Boeing 787 Dreamliner for London with a minute to spare and was sipping champagne and reading a Hiaasen novel ninety minutes after leaving home.

He had a two hour stopover next morning at London Airport, where he headed for American's Upper Class lounge. Who should be there but Carlton Tisch.

"Good morning," said Kon.

Tisch looked him up and down. Kon was wearing polo shirt, jeans and sneakers. Tisch himself was looking relatively smart. Mimi had made him wear a white linen suit, pointing out that he would be mixing with bankers, lawyers and other upper class criminals.

The lounge was quiet, unlike most of Heathrow. They ordered coffee, orange juice and eggs Benedict.

"What do we know?" asked Kon.

"Not much. Coward is missing. He doesn't answer his mobile. His hotel room was trashed. According to the waiter who brought him a bottle of Scotch around eleven the night before, a young Indian was with him. The waiter said he looked 'low class' – code for a rent boy. Now, neither hotel security nor the police can trace either of them."

"Are the Dubai police any good?"

Tisch shrugged. "Guess we'll find out."

66

Eight hours later, they were in Dubai. As their taxi from the airport approached the Burj al Thani Hotel, Kon eyed the dramatic, scimitar-shaped tower.

"Spectacular."

"Wait until you see inside. Some call it the most luxurious hotel in the world."

Upstairs, Kon walked round the 40th floor suite, admiring crystal mirrors and fingering the gold plated bathroom fittings.

"This is too much," he said. "It's over the top. I feel like stealing the faucets or throwing a rock through the window. Making a protest."

"Bad idea," said Carlton.

"You think?"

"The police will have your butt in a sling the minute you step out of line."

"Should I be scared?"

"Yes, you should. There are a lot of stories about the Dubai police. Does the name Len Adams mean anything to you?"

Kon shook his head.

"Len was a British tourist. He complained to the management of his hotel that a maid tried to steal some articles from his room. The police were called. There was an argument. It ended with him being arrested."

"For what?"

"For being disrespectful to the police."

"And was he?"

"I don't know, but he was denied bail."

Kon shrugged. "So he spent a week in jail."

"Six days actually."

"Then what?"

"He died."

"Died?"

Carlton nodded. "According to the police he became violent and had a heart attack. They promised to provide video showing it happening."

"Well then. Probably a troublemaker."

"We shall never know."

"Why?"

"Because they never released the video, despite the promises."

"I see your point."

"So the message is, treat the police with respect."

∾

Carlton wanted to get the facts about Coward's disappearance so he asked to meet the hotel manager. Half an hour later he and Kon were sitting in a conference room on the 26th floor enjoying a panoramic view of the bay, sipping mineral water and waiting for someone to appear.

"How will you play this?" asked Kon.

"By ear."

"Make it up as you go along, you mean?"

"Exactly."

The door opened. A tall man with fair hair and blue eyes walked in. Not your average Arab, thought Kon.

He looked them up and down and nodded. "Gunter Schmidt. Deputy manager."

"Just deputy?" said Carlton.

He's feeling aggressive, thought Kon, *that's not good.*

But Schmidt just smiled. "You will get better help from me. The manager, Shaikh Sulman bin Awali, is a cousin of the Ruler. He's a charming man, but day-to-day management is mostly left to me."

Carlton didn't like that, but he saw the sense of it. He sniffed.

Schmidt shrugged. "What do you want to know?"

Carlton nodded. "I am a colleague of Sir Paul Coward. We were partners."

"Partners?"

"In business."

"I don't know how much help I can be," said Schmidt. "The matter is in the hands of the police now. Are you a personal friend of Coward?"

"If you mean 'do I share his personal tastes,' no I do not."

There was silence in the room for a moment.

"Is being gay in Dubai a risky proposition?" asked Kon.

Schmidt shrugged. "It can be. Homosexual activity is illegal. Punishment can include prison, deportation, or even the death penalty."

Carlton said, "There are usually gay bars and an underground scene, even in places where the law is unfavourable."

"That's true here, too. The airlines are a significant factor, by the way."

"Because they bring gay visitors, you mean?"

"And their own employees."

Carlton said, "We think Coward's disappearance is the result of something more than a sexual disagreement."

Schmidt shrugged. "You may be right. I can only tell you what we know."

"Which is?"

"When the maid came next morning to clean the room, the "Do not disturb" sign was not posted so she went in. The place was a mess. Overturned furniture, blood on the carpet. No sign of Coward. It did not take a rocket scientist to suspect foul play. We called the police."

Kon, whose sense of humour tended to get him into trouble, was amused by the reference to rockets by this blue eyed German. "What happens now?" he asked. "Are the police investigating?"

Schmidt nodded. He produced a card and handed it to Carlton. "This is the inspector who came here. You can keep this, it's in our system."

Carlton examined the small white card. The printing was in Arabic.

"Turn it over," said Schmidt.

The other side was in English:

Detective Inspector Rashid bin Akbar, MBA (Columbia)
Al Twar, Dubai.

"Is the police station far away?" asked Carlton.

"Ten minutes by car."

Carlton got up. "Let's go."

"Good luck. Mind your manners with the police."

"Everyone says that," said Kon.

A smile played on Schmidt's lips. "Here's a cautionary tale, one of many: last year, a forty-four year old woman from Britain was arrested at Immigration and held in jail with her infant daughter. She was accused of drinking a single glass of wine – provided free, ironically, by Emirates Airlines which is state-owned."

"She was locked up?"

"With her daughter. Jail conditions were dreadful. She was treated roughly, denied access to a toilet, the child had to urinate on the floor."

"Was she drunk?"

"No, but her visa had expired. She may have been disrespectful to the immigration people. Depends who you believe."

"What happened?"

"After several days of media coverage in the British

tabloids, the Ruler intervened. He overruled Immigration and the charges were dropped. But it cost the woman thousands of dollars in legal fees, not to mention the stress."

Kon was listening. A year ago he had spent four days without food, tortured and close to death, in a three foot square cell in Cuba.

Carlton thanked Schmidt. "We'll be careful."

Damn right, thought Kon.

67

I n Guinea-Malia, Basil Heinie took a taxi to the airport for his flight to Dubai. He was pleased with the progress he had made. The next few weeks should be dramatically profitable.

But he must handle things carefully, especially his relationship with Shiv Bosu.

He was not always frank with the Bosus, in fact he lied comprehensively on certain subjects. He justified this to himself without difficulty. He had prospered greatly over the years while working for Shiv, who paid him several times what he could have earned in a more conventional company, but he was not grateful. Gratitude was not in his personality. And there was another problem, for which there was no solution: *he was not family*.

Shiv Bosu was usually polite but the other brothers sneered behind his back, he had overheard them. He knew very well that if things got tight they would drop him like a red hot yam. He must always be ready to fire them before they fired him. Someone said only the paranoid survive and, whoever it was, they were right. It was a matter of survival.

So he had a private agenda, especially about events in Guinea-Malia which were now well advanced. There was money to be made there, clearly, and that money must flow to Heinie, not the Bosus. It was only fair. Heinie, not Shiv, had initiated discussions with the country's President and he intended to keep things that way. He had been waiting a long time for a chance to cut loose from Bosu for good, and with a huge payday. Recent meetings with the brothers had not improved his mood and the resentment of years was ready to boil over, but if he played his cards right all insults would shortly be avenged.

The Guinea-Malia project involved Bosu-style state capture again, he reflected, but with a variation. Bribing the President was not the key, but misleading him was.

The old fool was obsessed with improving the profitability of the country's copper mines, ignoring the fact that low world prices, not management, were the problem, and Heinie was elated at having persuaded him that computerised accounting equipment would cure all ills. Once installed, it would enable Heinie to hack into the system and siphon out the operation's cash. He had already formed a corporation and opened a bank account under a different name to conceal his plans from the Bosus. They would have no idea what was happening until it was too late. Shiv's obvious suspicion in their telephone conversation was worrying – it sounded as if a final confrontation might be near – but even if it happened, the deed would be done by then and the money safe.

He checked the calendar on his mobile phone. As he was doing so, a message flashed on his screen.

It said, simply:

Subject: Coward

Status: relocated – see text message

The message was from a commercial espionage agency, a service available on the Dark Web which he used to monitor the movements of key players in Bosu's projects. Those players did not include Carlton Tisch, who he considered merely a passive investor, but he did receive daily updates on Sir Paul Coward, based on phone signals and credit card activity, so he always knew where the Britisher was.

He checked his text messages and learned that Coward was heading to Dubai. He had no idea why but it was useful to know, good intel was never wasted. He had met Coward briefly when the project was being set up and had not warmed to him. He suspected the feeling was mutual, and he had made a note back then to monitor Coward's movements more closely.

Arriving in Dubai after the long flight he took a taxi to the mansion in Emirates Hills owned by the Bosus. When he got to the house he checked his texts again and there was one from the tracer service saying that Sir Paul Coward was at the Burj al Thani Hotel.

So, within minutes of Coward checking into his hotel, Heinie knew he was there and was considering what to do about it.

68

Carlton and Kon took a taxi to the Al Ahram police station. It was a white modern building. Two million dollars of sleek Bugatti Veyron in the green and white of the Dubai Police sat in the sunshine outside.

A young Arab of medium height came and shook hands with Carlton and Kon. He smiled pleasantly. "Rashid."

His face was smooth, with a neat black beard. He looked about thirty. He wore a full length white burnous and an Arab headdress with a gold band.

"First question," said Kon. "Is that your Veyron?"

"It belongs to the people of Dubai, but I drive it."

"Top speed 250 miles per hour?"

"We also have a Bentley Continental, an Aston Martin and three Porsches."

"Those are pretty expensive for cop cars," said Carlton.

"They're not really for chasing bad guys. It's more of a PR thing, a way to connect with people."

"Better than connecting by arresting them, I guess," said Kon.

Rashid smiled uncertainly.

Carlton raised a hand.

"We're here because of the disappearance of Paul Coward. It's possible we can help."

Rashid looked at him. "I don't understand. With respect, who are you and why would we need your help?"

Carlton said, "Coward's presence in Dubai is because of our investment – his and mine – in South Africa. Are you familiar with what is going on there?"

"So-called 'state capture?'"

Carlton nodded. "With the proceeds being siphoned to Dubai."

"What does Coward have to do with that?"

Carlton explained about Bosu Construction and its low-cost housing project.

Rashid listened carefully. "How is Mr. Coward involved?"

"He came to Dubai to follow the money trail in respect of $35 million of fraudulently converted funds."

"But why kidnap him?"

"The Bosus have had a great run in South Africa, stealing millions of dollars, but it's coming to an end. Lawsuits loom, cash is dwindling, newspapers are snapping at their heels. We think they are getting desperate, panicking and willing to use violence."

"On Coward?"

"Possibly. Coward is a smart guy. His personal life may be reckless but he's as sharp as a tack and the Bosus don't know what he might discover. With his banking knowledge he might trace the Bosus' money and even get it frozen."

Rashid nodded. "I understand what you say. But frankly our resources here are limited. We can't run the sort of investigation that would be mounted in London or New York."

"What *have* you done?" asked Kon.

"We checked the hotel's phone records. Coward made a number of calls when he arrived, mostly to dating agencies. The last one was to a gay bar."

"I thought Dubai did not tolerate such things?"

"That is true – officially. But everything is for sale and there is plenty of money here. Plus a certain flexibility among the police."

"You mean corruption," said Kon.

Carlton cut him off. "So you have a lead – the bar. Have you followed it up?"

Rashid shook his head.

"May I ask why?"

He shrugged. "Lack of manpower."

"Not enough people to follow up a kidnapping?" asked Kon.

"We have a tiny population."

"Three million is not tiny," said Carlton. He lived on an island with only 24,000 inhabitants.

"Less than half a million are Arabs like me. The rest are expatriates, mainly from India and Pakistan."

"If you are short handed, perhaps you won't mind us looking around by ourselves?"

Rashid looked doubtful. "I can't stop you. But you would have to report to me and keep me informed."

"Don't worry, we'll see you get full credit. I see your MBA is from Columbia. We New Yorkers should stick together."

"What was the name of the bar?" Kon asked.

"The Pink Champagne."

~

The Pink Champagne was in a nondescript alley near Mushrif Park, out toward the airport.

Bright sunshine gave way abruptly to near darkness as Kon and Carlton went inside. They sat at the bar, trying to get accustomed to the gloom.

It was only mid morning but the scene was jumping. Casually dressed couples danced to deafening music, some with arms wrapped around one another in the chilly air conditioning, others more discreet. The smell of sweat was palpable.

"What'll it be?" The barman looked oriental but the voice was East Coast U.S.A.

"A Cuba Libre," said Carlton.

"And for your young friend?"

Kon blinked, then realised they had been mistaken for a gay couple. In a place like this, what else? He was about to protest but Carlton put a limp hand on his arm.

"Kon's too young for alcohol, aren't you Konnie. He'll have a Shirley Temple."

Kon hid a look of disgust.

When their drinks arrived, Carlton asked the bartender. "Has Aziz been in?"

"What's it to you?"

"We heard he was up for some fun."

"What sort of fun?"

Carlton contrived a blush. "Threesome fun."

The bartender shrugged. "He's in and out. Not for a couple of days, though. He seems to have gone quiet – some kind of trouble at the Burj al Thani."

"If you see him, tell him we'd like to get together. He'll find it worth his while. This is Kon and I'm Carl. Here's my mobile." Carlton scribbled on a scrap of paper and handed it to the barman.

"I'll see what I can do."

They left. Outside, Kon said, "What now?"

"We wait."

"At least you didn't ask me to dance."

69

At Dubai Airport, two muscular looking Indians, Johan and Gordo, descended from the Air India Airbus. They had flown business class but did not fit the part, being rough-featured and appearing uncomfortable in new-looking suits.

They moved swiftly through the business lane, past immigration and customs and stood waiting on the sidewalk.

"Where's the frigging limo?" demanded Johan, the taller of the two.

"They said it would be here," muttered his stocky companion. He produced an iPhone and called the Bosu villa.

"Where's our vehicle?"

The girl at the villa, a Palestine Arab, said, "Nobody told us you were coming."

"Send it now," he snapped.

She didn't like his tone. "Get a taxi, it's just as quick."

They complied, grumbling.

Arriving at the villa, they dumped their luggage roughly on an antique table in the elegant lounge. From his bag Johan took two identical white plastic objects about four inches long and laid them side by side on the polished surface.

Gordo followed suit, producing objects of a different shape. Johan carefully mated each object to its partner and hefted each of the resulting pistols in his hand.

The door opened and Heinie entered the room. He eyed the white automatics and smiled faintly.

"Two plastic firearms in perfect working order, of no interest to airport security, either in India or Dubai," said Johan.

Heinie sat down and motioned the others to sit too. "Coffee?"

"I'd prefer something stronger," said Johan.

Heinie shook his head. "No alcohol in Dubai."

Johan looked disappointed. "Not even in a private house? That's absurd."

"Maybe. But Bosu's operation in Dubai is cleaner than clean. We are in a decent upper class area, not the Mumbai slums. You are honest citizens, moving in respectable circles. Remember that."

He produced two VISA cards and gave one to each man.

"You can sign for everything. Dress conservatively and don't drink or misbehave."

"Except . . ." Gordo leered and indicated the firearms.

Heinie shrugged. "Obviously."

"So what's the project?" asked Johan.

Heinie produced a photograph. "It includes this man."

The photo showed Carlton Tisch, looking formal in a dark suit and tie. It could have been clipped from the Wall Street Journal or a company annual report.

"He's our target?" asked Johan.

"One of them. There are two others, an Israeli and an Indian."

"They said in Mumbai there were two white guys to be eliminated," said Gordo.

"That's correct."

"So why the Indian?"

Heinie shrugged. "He knows about the other two. Best to wipe the slate clean."

Gordo nodded.

"Glad you approve," said Heinie.

"Where do we start?"

"The white men are at the Burj al Thani Hotel."

"The smart joint with the helicopter pad?"

"Just so. One other thing." Heinie produced two mobile phones. "These are pre-loaded with more credit than you will need." He handed one to each man. "Return them to me when you are done."

Johan got up, motioned to Gordo. "Let's get to work."

70

J ohan and Gordo rented a car, a grey Camry, and drove to the Burj al Thani where they left the vehicle with the valet and sat in the lobby sipping lemonade. Gordo pretended to read the Dubai Lonely Planet guide. They were actually studying the guests and comparing them to Heinie's photograph.

Nothing happened for an hour. Then Carlton Tisch and Kon Feaver emerged from the elevator and walked across the lobby toward the front entrance. Gordo and Johan recognised Tisch from his photo and followed them outside.

Carlton and Kon got into a cab. Gordo and Johan had no time to fetch their car so they hailed another taxi.

"Follow that cab," Gordo ordered.

"Just like in the movies," said the driver, a young Muslim in long white *thobe* and embroidered cap.

Johan scowled. "Where are you from?"

"Bangladesh."

"Well, Bangladesh, do as you're told and I won't break your face."

"No need to be hostile." They followed the cab in silence.

It was a short ride, ending at the local Hertz Rent-a-Car office.

"Pull over and wait," snapped Gordo.

"I charge for waiting," said the driver.

Gordo gave him a look and he shut up.

71

Carlton and Kon were in the Hertz office.

"We need a car," said Kon.

"Yes, sir, what kind?"

Kon caught Carlton's eye. "The most expensive," Carlton had an obsession with wanting the best of everything, and equated 'best' with 'most expensive.' It was a hang-up from his youth in New York's Lower East Side.

"We have a Lexus ES350 automatic."

"Anything with a bit more punch?"

"There's a Dodge Challenger. That's in our 'Fun' range."

"Do you have a Rolls?" asked Carlton.

"No, sir. Most customers are very happy with the Lexus."

Carl scowled at Kon. "We're in the wrong place. Use your mobile phone, go on the internet and look for a Rolls."

Kon had been through this before. He keyed "Rolls Royce" into the phone but nothing came up.

"How about a BMW 7 series?" said the dealer. "Only $250 a day."

"That's expensive," said Kon.

Carlton frowned. "I guess we may have to take it."

"Hold on," said Kon, "Here's something. Paddock Rentals. They have several Rolls Royces. Do you want a Phantom, a Dawn, a Wraith or a Ghost? They're all about a thousand bucks a day. There's also a yellow Bentley Mulsanne that looks pretty cool."

Carlton shook his head. "Has to be a Rolls." He looked over Kon's shoulder. "I see a Rolls Cullinan, an SUV – that looks interesting."

"Why do you need an SUV? You're not going off road."

"How do you know? Could be useful in the sand dunes."

"What dunes? And there's no price listed."

Carlton shook his head. "Let's go round there."

Half an hour later they were seated in the biggest, heaviest Rolls Kon had ever seen. It weighed almost three tons and looked as if it would sink up to its axles in any sand but that didn't matter because Carlton was satisfied.

"Take her away," he told Kon, who was driving.

"Where to?"

"Anywhere. The desert."

"If we head north east on the coast road we should reach Ras al-Khaimah in about an hour."

"What is that?"

"It's another of the Emirates, much smaller than Dubai. It's somewhere to drive."

The ride in the Rolls was near-silent and as smooth as silk.

Gordo and Johan were not far behind in their taxi. The driver had no experience of following other cars without being seen and, anxious to oblige Johan and Gordo, he got pretty close to the Rolls.

In front of them, Kon was enjoying driving the luxurious SUV, but after a few minutes he noticed the cab in his rear view mirror and pointed it out to Carlton.

Carlton craned his neck. "Two people on board."

"Anyone we know?"

"No, but they are probably not our friends."

"What should we do about it?"

"Nothing," said Carlton after a moment's thought. "But I'm starting to think we may be seriously outnumbered,"

"That's not good is it?"

"No it's not."

72

Carlton's mobile phone rang.

"Hello?"

"This is Aziz. You left a message at the Pink Champagne." A slight Indian accent.

"Hi, Aziz. It's really nice to hear from you." Carlton was effusive, not his normal curt self.

"How can I help you?"

"My friend Kon and I are in town for a few days. We're looking for a good time."

"That's fine, but how do I know who you are?"

"Isn't that an occupational risk?"

"I guess we could meet."

"Now you're talking."

There was a pause on the line. "Be at Starbucks in the Mall of the Emirates in half an hour. I'm wearing white jeans and a pink polo."

"Sounds fetching."

"There are four Starbucks in the Mall. You want the one at ground level."

"Okay. See you."

~

"A bit cloak and dagger, isn't he?" said Kon.

"I don't blame him. So would you be, in his business."

"I guess Ras al-Khaimah will have to wait."

73

The sun scorched their faces as they walked the few feet from their taxi to the Mall entrance, but inside the huge place was ice-cold.

They could just as well have been in the United States. There were rows of high-end stores including Tiffany and Macys. Their route to Starbucks took them through the women's shoe department of Neiman Marcus.

"Notice anything about this stuff?" Kon asked Carlton.

The little New Yorker shook his head.

"I don't see anything under $600."

Starbucks was empty apart from a young Indian.

"Aziz?"

He nodded warily.

There was an awkward silence, broken by Kon. "Well, since we're in Starbucks we'd better order something."

They sipped their drinks. Aziz cleared his throat. "You don't look like candidates for my services."

"You noticed that?" said Kon.

"Let's call a spade a spade," said Carlton. "You seem a smart young man. Why do you think we're here?"

"I can't imagine."

"A certain person is missing from a suite at the Burj al Thani."

"I've no idea what you mean." Aziz's gaze swivelled toward the restaurant entrance.

"Don't pretend you don't know," snapped Carlton. "And don't try and run. I'm not young any more but my companion is a good athlete, you wouldn't get far."

Aziz sat back with a sigh. "I suppose you are talking about the Englishman, Paul. Are you friends of his?"

Carlton nodded.

"We spent a pleasant evening, what can I say? I'm surprised he's missing."

"You're saying you didn't know?"

"That's right."

"Any comment?"

Aziz shrugged. "I'm sorry if he's your friend but it's not my problem. He was in good spirits when I left. I might even say he had an air of quiet satisfaction."

"There was blood in the room," said Carlton. "The police are investigating. You will have to tell them you were there."

"Why?"

"Because if you don't I shall."

"I don't want to get involved. Not as a witness, and certainly not as a suspect."

"You are involved already, young man!"

Aziz thought for a minute, then frowned. "I suppose I only have two choices, to check in with the police, or to get out of Dubai. But the thing is, my livelihood is here. What would you do in my place?"

Carlton shook his head. "Not my problem, to use your words. So you have no idea what happened to Coward?"

"Absolutely none." He stood up.

"We may need to speak to you again."

Aziz shrugged, then reached in his pocket and produced a card. "This number will reach me." He turned and walked out of the coffee shop.

Carlton watched him leave, then turned to Kon. "What do you think? Do you believe him?"

"I would like to," said Kon. "He didn't talk like a killer."

"He's not clean," said Carlton.

"You think? Why?"

"He's shifty."

"So are a million other people."

"I just have a feeling."

"What do we do next? We can't tap his phone."

"We can follow him," said Carlton.

"By 'we,' I suppose you mean me," said Kon.

"That's right." Carlton handed him Aziz's card.

Kon grabbed his half-finished Pepsi and hurried out of the mall.

74

Kon sat in the Rolls outside Aziz's apartment. He kept the engine running for the sake of the air conditioning. He was sipping the remains of his drink from Starbucks. It had been cold originally but was now unappetisingly warm.

He had been there for two hours, waiting for Aziz to reappear. He was annoyed at Carlton for posting him here, even though he realised the older man was not a good surveillance candidate himself.

His hope of seeing Aziz emerge was dwindling. He took out his phone and called Carlton.

"What's happening?" asked Carlton.

"Nothing. I should have brought a book."

But at that moment the front door opened and out stepped Aziz. He marched across the parking area and climbed into his car, a white Range Rover.

Nice wheels for a working guy, Kon thought.

He pulled out and followed him. The Range Rover

headed toward downtown Dubai. Kon fell in behind at a discreet distance. Anywhere else, driving a Rolls Royce would have been conspicuous but this was Dubai and in the space of ten minutes he passed another Rolls and two Bentleys coming the other way.

He thought at first that Aziz was going back to the Burj al Thani. But this time it was the Jumeirah Beach Hotel, also modern and, by the look of things, expensive even by Dubai standards. Aziz handed the Range Rover keys to a valet and went in so Kon did the same, following Aziz inside.

He knows what I look like, so be careful, he thought. He peered around the spacious, ultra-modern lounge. No sign of Aziz. He tried the bar, and there was the young Indian. He was sitting at a table talking to a man in his fifties in a lightweight tan suit. The bar was dimly lit and had pillars at intervals, so Kon was able to find a table where he had a view of Aziz and his companion but was himself shielded behind a column.

The man in the suit was grey haired and taut faced. He looked anxious, his thin mouth turned down at the corners. He was talking volubly and seemed annoyed. Aziz replied, gesticulating. Or negotiating, because the man reached in his jacket pocket and produced a brown envelope, letter-sized but fat. He handed it to Aziz. *Sure looks like money,* thought Kon.

He whipped out his phone, put it in camera mode and, holding it up above his shoulder, took a picture of the two men. He took a second picture as insurance. There was not much more he could do without becoming conspicuous, so not wishing to push his luck he got up and slipped away without being seen.

In the lobby he found a quiet corner and phoned Carlton.

"Who was the guy?" Carlton asked.

"Nobody I know. But I have pictures."

"On your phone?"

"Yes."

"Send me a photo. Do you know how to do that?"

After some fumbling, Kon managed to attach the better of the two pictures to a text message and send it to Carlton. Carlton called back immediately.

"I know that man."

"Who is it?"

"Basil Heinie. He's the Bosus' financial guy. A South African, but based here in Dubai."

"Small world, eh? What should I do next?"

"Nothing. Get out of there."

"Shouldn't I follow them or something?"

"There's no point. You know what this means, don't you?"

"Uh . . ."

Impatiently Carlton said, "Basil Heinie had Coward snatched, and may have had him killed. Aziz did the kidnapping, for money. There's no other explanation."

75

By now it was obvious to Carlton that he and Kon needed all the support they could get. His next call was to Oliver in Johannesburg.

He described the day's events. "Heinie is here and I'm pretty sure he has some strong-arm help, probably goons from Bosu's operation in Mumbai. So we need you. This is where the action is."

"We're on our way, just as soon as we can get a flight. What's the story with Paul Coward?"

"I assume he is either a captive or dead. If he's still alive he's probably a prisoner in the Bosu mansion."

"We may have to go in there," said Oliver.

∿

We flew to Dubai – Ron Halfshaft, Omar Sen and me. The flight took eight hours.

Ron and I were in business class but Omar insisted

on flying first class. I found this surprising, since he had been bending my ear about how expensive life was – the fare in first class was three times business and ten times economy – but he said it was important for his image. "What if I bumped into one of my bridge partners and he was in first while I was slumming it in business?"

"Oh the shame of it," I said.

Omar frowned. "It's all about perceptions."

"Whatever."

Anyway, we reunited at Dubai where to my surprise a white limousine met our plane and drove us to the Yacht Marina.

The limo driver walked with us to a private security gate where he punched in a five digit key code allowing us onto the jetty. There, Omar's yacht Ariadne was moored. She was as large as a decent sized house. I thought at first she was a triple decker because of the rows of windows on three levels, but then I realised there were portholes in the black-painted lower sides as well, suggesting there were at least five floors not counting the bilges, whatever those are.

On a dedicated flat area in the rear sat a helicopter, securely fastened to hooks in the deck. It was red and shiny, with room for four passengers and a pilot.

Omar ushered us up the gangway. "Welcome aboard."

I nodded at him. "This is very nice. But a helicopter? Really?"

He shrugged. "A small one. It came with the boat."

A blonde appeared. Not a dumb blonde, though.

Smart in fact, smiling and in her twenties. She wore a blue and white striped tee shirt and black shorts.

"This is Gay, she arranged the limo. She'll show you to your cabins," said Omar. "Come aft when you've settled in and we'll make plans."

"Welcome," said Gay. "Let's go this way. Holler if you need anything. There's Wi-fi everywhere, no password needed."

"She came with the boat, too," muttered Omar, looking embarrassed.

I was expecting a compact cabin but not a bit of it, there was plenty of space, equivalent to a good sized Hilton bedroom and with similar amenities, including its own bathroom, a Keurig coffee maker and charging points for computer and mobile phone. Unlike at Hilton, there were silk curtains and spruce panelling and the bathroom fittings were gold or something like it.

Halfshaft had the cabin next to mine. After a few minutes he knocked on the door. "Do you think they have room service?"

"Probably. But we should go and talk business."

We headed upstairs. He was carrying his laptop.

"Do you take that thing everywhere?" I asked.

"Except in the shower."

"Most people use tablets. They are lighter."

"Toys," he scoffed. "This is the real thing. It contains a bunch of stuff I wrote myself."

"Stuff for what?"

"Searching."

"Searching for what?"

"Anything."

"Is that useful?"

"You'll see."

~

We reclined on deck in canvas chairs. A contraption blew dry air at us, offsetting the humid surroundings. The temperature, in the forties centigrade during the day, had fallen to an almost bearable thirty.

Omar turned out to be a dry martini person. I asked Gay if she could fix a *mojito*. She frowned as if I had asked her if she could boil water and when it arrived it was as strong as I've ever tasted.

The phone rang. It was Carlton from the Burj al Thani. "We're coming round." Minutes later, a taxi drew up at the jetty and disgorged him and Kon.

Carlton and Omar had never met, so I introduced them. The New York financier and the Pakistani bridge champion shook hands. Carlton gazed around.

"Is this yours?"

Omar smiled. "For my sins. Are you a yachtsman?"

"After a fashion. Do you sail?"

It was a barbed question. Carlton has won the over-fifty round-the-island race on Tortola in a twenty-footer, three times. There was salt under his fingernails and probably in his DNA. Also, if he wanted, he could afford to put down a hundred million for a much bigger boat than Ariadne. He was not going to defer to some dude who won a luxury cabin cruiser playing bridge.

Omar ignored the question. "Let me get you a drink."

Carlton opted for beer. He sipped from the can and Kon did the same, to Omar's frowning disapproval.

I had wondered how Omar and Carlton would get on. Two smart guys, both with big egos. Omar was rich, but Carlton was richer by a Virgin Island mile. That could be a recipe for a major personality clash and at first I was afraid it might happen, but the atmosphere soon mellowed.

As we sipped our drinks, I realised the odd man out in this group was yours truly. I was sitting with a bridge grand master, a Wall Street tycoon and a computer geek with perfect memory. I felt inadequate. But I've never let my own inadequacy bother me, so I dealt with it.

From where we sat we could see the lofty outline of the Burj al Thani. I indicated the leaf shaped helipad near its summit. "Can you fly a helicopter directly from here to the hotel?"

Omar laughed. "Yes, and I did that a couple of times for supper, but it soon gets old. Helicopters are very noisy."

"I can see how it must cost a packet to keep this show going."

"As I said, a million a year including maintenance, mooring fees and salaries for the crew. That's why I have to keep playing bridge with very rich people."

"My heart bleeds," I said.

He smiled. "This is quite small, as yachts go."

"Really?"

"The vessel Octopus, which belonged to the late Paul

Allen of Microsoft, is 414 feet long and has a crew of fifty-seven. That's large."

"With helicopter, of course?"

"Two. And a submarine."

"Point taken," I said. "Now, to business. Our goal is to find the Bosus' headquarters, free Paul Coward and make Shiv Bosu account for the murder of Lucy Gray and other crimes."

"We know where his house is," said Carlton.

"House? There are houses as well as apartments in Dubai?"

"Sure. They are expensive, of course. In the Emirates Hills district, you're talking eight figures."

"Is that where he is based?"

Carlton nodded. "He has a huge villa, 24,000 square feet on a two acre lot. It has twelve bedrooms, twelve bathrooms and a big pool. He paid $40 million and then spent another $10 million upgrading it and – note this – fortifying it."

"Easy to break into, then," I said.

"I agree," said Kon.

"I was kidding," I said.

He grinned. "I wasn't."

Omar said, "You don't want to behave recklessly in Dubai. Don't be fooled by those flashy police cars which are mostly for show. There are real police here and they don't take kindly to visitors who ignore the law."

"What can they do?" asked Kon.

Omar looked at him. "Anything they want. You may have heard that they arrested a woman and her child arriving from Britain because she drank a glass of wine that was served free by the state airline. The police did not like her attitude."

"I heard about that. But wasn't she offending in some other way?"

"Who knows? The point is, be *really* careful!"

"Carlton is rich, he can buy his way out of trouble," said Kon. "It's a pity we're not armed, though."

Carlton and I exchanged glances. We had been around Kon for a while and knew how he thought. He was capable of senseless violence in a good cause. That worried us both.

"We need a plan," said Carlton.

Omar was listening. "In spades," he said.

I n Johannesburg, Shiv Bosu's pilot Jake was waiting with engines warmed up and ready to go in the area of O.R.Tambo Airport reserved for private aircraft. The 'plane was airborne within fifteen minutes of Shiv's arrival.

They climbed through light cloud to twenty thousand feet. Shiv loosened his seat belt, exhaled and sat back in his seat.

For the first time in days he relaxed, and even congratulated himself. He was out of South Africa. By the skin of his teeth perhaps, but out. He was leaving behind two brothers, one dead and the other in prison for murder. He was abandoning companies worth over a billion dollars at normal valuation although, given the circumstances, probably much less. It was a bitter pill to swallow. But at least he was safe.

The aircraft, a Bombardier BD 700 Global Express built for eighteen passengers, had been re-fitted throughout to his personal taste. The main cabin contained a sofa, a rosewood table and six cream leather chairs. There was gold trim and polished wood everywhere. A master bedroom suite with a double bed was next door. There was a bathroom with gold-plated faucets and shower. The modern kitchen included a refrigerator, oven and every known stainless steel appliance.

The airplane could cruise at 500 knots on its two Rolls Royce engines, with a stated range of 5,750 miles. Dubai was 5,600 miles away so in theory they could get there without stopping. However, the distance was uncomfortably close to the plane's maximum range. Shiv was a gambler in business but when it came to his own safety he was very cautious so he decided to make a stop along the way. His sense of freedom on leaving South Africa made him almost light-headed and in his euphoria he was in no particular hurry to get to Dubai, so he decided to spend a day in Harare, the capital of Zimbabwe.

He had a particular motive for stopping in the former Salisbury, the capital of what had once been Rhodesia. He had developed a highly profitable relationship with one Gabriel Mutapa, minister without portfolio in the cabinet of Emmerson Mnangagwa who had succeeded the senile nonagenarian Mugabe. The details were complicated but, in essence, a company controlled by Shiv via an offshore subsidiary had landed a contract to build and manage prisons in the country. Payment would be in US dollars and everything was looking good but it wouldn't hurt to spend a little time reassuring Mutapa of their friendship and reminding him, literally, where his next dollar was coming from. So Shiv checked into Meikles Hotel in Harare and spent an agreeable evening wining and dining Gabriel in a quiet corner of the elegant La Fontaine Grill Room. Satisfied that all was in order, he bade the amenable minister farewell and, next day, he and Jake were off again.

It was nearly midnight by the time they reached Dubai.

∾

Basil Heinie was on the tarmac to greet him.

"What's the story with Paul Coward?" asked Shiv.

"We have him in custody at the villa. But there's a problem."

"What's that?"

"Oliver Steele is here. So are Carlton Tisch and his sidekick, Feaver."

Shiv looked puzzled. "When I left Joburg, Steele was still there."

"Maybe so. He and his friends Halfshaft and Sen must have left shortly after you, and flown here direct while you spent the night in Harare."

Shiv scowled. "I suppose so. Anyway, we should eliminate them all."

Even Heinie looked shocked, but Shiv just shrugged wearily. He was tired from travel and regretted making the remark but at this stage he felt ready to do whatever was necessary to safeguard himself and his fortune.

They got into Heinie's white Jaguar and in minutes arrived at the Bosu residence.

It was one of the biggest houses in Dubai. A colonnaded entrance led to the central lobby which had an imposing open staircase to the upper floor. Huge windows extended the full two story height of the building, providing dramatic views across a large swimming pool towards the ocean. It presented a dazzling vista of stars against the blue-black night sky.

"Where are Steele and his friends staying?" Shiv asked.

"On Omar Sen's yacht in the Marina."

77

"**N**ow, Basil, let's *really* talk," said Shiv Bosu.

They were in the room Bosu used as his office.

They were coming to the end of an hour long session in which the accountant had summarised the activity of each of Bosu's companies around the world – its sales, profits and how much cash it had generated in the past month.

"About?"

"About your activity in Guinea-Malia."

Shiv smiled but the smile was limited to his full lips. The piercing brown eyes remained cold.

Heinie was in an upright chair across the desk from the plump faced Indian. He thought about making an excuse and leaving and he stood up, but the door was blocked by the impassive Johan who had an AK47 slung over his shoulder. He shuffled his feet and sat down.

Bosu nodded. "So, Guinea-Malia!"

"Yes, boss."

"I'm a bit concerned by your behaviour. You showed initiative – I like that, initiative is good – but you know what else is good?"

"What, boss?"

"Transparency. I like to know everything that's going on in my little empire." He coughed modestly. "Did I say empire? A rather grand word but you know what I mean."

"Of course." Heinie glanced at Johan who moved forward, smiling, and swung his weapon in Heinie's direction. Heinie recoiled, then recovered his balance. When he realised Johan was not going to attack him, he laughed nervously.

"Tell me again, what were you going to do with the copper money when it arrived?"

"Why, transfer it to one of your accounts."

Bosu smiled. "Good. Go on."

"Yes. In fact, I was about to ask which account to send it to. Should I use a corporate account, or an account in your own name? Stuff like that." He was babbling now.

Bosu waved a hand. "That's all detail. Let's talk again when you are ready to make the transfer."

"Of course."

"When will that be, by the way?"

"A week tomorrow. That's when China's promissory note matures."

"Good. We can discuss it then."

Their eyes met. The exchange was brief, but Heinie was in no doubt he had been given a warning. Now he was unsure of his position. He had not been fired, but how much trust remained in the reservoir that he had spent years building?

Well okay, he thought, it had been optimistic to hope Bosu would ever trust anyone outside his family. If he even trusted them.

"Thank you, boss, thank you very much."

Bosu waved in dismissal.

Heinie glanced at Johan. Johan leered but stood aside and let him stumble from the room.

78

On the yacht, Carlton and Omar's announcement about the need for a plan was met with silence. Everyone waited for someone else to provide useful input.

"Planning?" I said finally. "Yes. Well I hate to talk like an accountant, but let's review our strengths and weaknesses. First, our strengths: Financial. We have money."

"So do they," said Kon.

"We don't have weapons," I said.

"They do, you can be sure," said Carlton.

"That's a weakness then."

"We have manpower," said Ron.

"Really?"

"There are five of us. Six if you count Gay."

Omar said, "We also have the assistance of a gentleman called Hassan. Hassan is our 'fixer' here in UAE. He is a native of Dubai and he is in every business you can think of, from construction to boat repair to getting licenses for this and that. He also has a contact, usually a cousin, in every branch of local government. In a place like Dubai, having a Hassan is essential."

"I hope you cultivate him," I said.

"Of course. Gay makes a point of being extra nice."

"But they probably still outnumber us," said Carlton. "Who knows how many people there are in that villa."

"Our people are smarter," said Kon. "I think."

"Don't be so sure," I said. "Shiv Bosu is very clever. You may not like his methods, but the way he systematically extracted money from Protea was pretty brilliant."

Ron said, "This place, his villa. What do we know about it?"

"We know where it is, and that it's a big building. That's about all," said Omar.

"What's the address?"

"1077 Paradise Road, Emirates Hills."

"How long have they owned it?"

"About two years."

"Then there should still be records on the estate agent's website." He opened his laptop, nodding at me. "See what I mean?"

He keyed in the villa's address and in moments up came the website of the real estate agent that had advertised the house.

The photo showed a long two storey building and a large pool with trees on either side. The scale was hard to gauge but to me the place looked the size of Buckingham Palace. It was flagged as "Sold."

Kon whistled. "That sucker is big."

Ron was typing. "There's some more detail here. It was archived when the sale went through but I may be able to bring it back."

Moments later he brought up a screen full of information.

"Here it is."

I looked over his shoulder. "Twelve bedrooms, twelve bathrooms, three kitchens. *Three* kitchens?"

Kon laughed. "One may be for the help."

"I think I read about this place," said Carlton. "The previous owner was Sachs, a Jewish banker from Beirut. He was quite orthodox, so one of the kitchens may have been kosher."

"Odd place for a Jew to live," I said.

Carlton nodded. "It is unusual. But the UAE prides itself on its religious tolerance. There's a small Jewish community here – people in the diamond trade, things like that. There's even a synagogue, although it's in a rented villa and they keep the address quiet in case of terrorism.

I read on, "Bowling alley, conservatory, pool house with his-and-hers locker rooms. Library, projection room . . ."

"I get the idea," said Kon. "It's big."

"But how many people? We should go and take a look, observe them coming and going," I said.

"You mean drive there and lie in wait, watch them from the car?"

"For starters." I was not wildly enthusiastic, but nobody seemed to have a better idea.

"So is that the plan?" asked Omar.

"Few plans survive the sound of the first gunfire," said Carlton drily.

~

Next morning, Kon and I got in my car and we drove to Emirates Hills. I had rented a silver Infiniti G37 and was pleased with its sporty acceleration and handling.

Ron followed us. He too had rented a car, a Ford Fiesta. "What's the plan?" he asked.

"Kon and I are the primary watchers. You hang back. If something happens, we'll phone you instructions."

"What sort of instructions?"

"I'll tell you then."

"In other words, you have no idea," said Ron.

"It's called being flexible."

Paradise Road was tree-lined, the grass and hedges well watered, clearly a high rent area. It reminded me of the region around Palm Springs in Southern California – hot, dry and totally dependent on irrigation.

At number 1077, massive iron gates faced the road A smoothly raked gravel drive curved away out of sight behind bushes so that we could not see the house itself.

We stopped by the side of the road and waited. After a quarter of an hour, Kon yawned. "How long are we supposed to hang about like this?"

"Until something happens." I said, irritated. He knew the plan, he was just being awkward.

Five minutes later the gates swung open, powered

remotely. Out came a grey Ford truck with a four door cabin. The driver and passenger were both heavy-set men and we glimpsed their impassive faces as the vehicle swept by.

"They look like the enforcers," said Kon. "I wonder where they're going. Shall we follow them?"

I shook my head. "No. Someone else might emerge. We're here to watch today."

"Boring," muttered Kon.

"I have a better idea." I reached for my phone and called Ron. "Where are you?"

"In a side street facing onto Paradise Road, half a mile behind you, just like you said."

"Watch out for a grey truck with two large body-guards in it."

"How do you know they're bodyguards?"

"I don't, not for sure, but that's how they look."

Ron interrupted. "Hold on, here it comes. Yeah, I see what you mean about the guys. Rough."

"That's them."

"What shall I do?"

"Follow them. See where they go."

"Roger that."

"Don't let yourself be seen. If they spot you and get suspicious we would lose the element of surprise, one of our few advantages."

"Got it." He rang off.

I was not too happy about Ron. He had plenty of enthusiasm, but that was both a strength and a weakness. He lacked subtlety. What sort of a job would he make of tailing suspects, a task that called for finesse? But there wasn't much I could do except trust him.

Kon and I settled down to wait. Half an hour later, a sleek white Mercedes appeared and the gates swung open again to let it out. It was driven by a tan suited individual, alone. He was skinny and looked somewhat intense but otherwise his appearance offered few clues. He could have been anything from a butler to a company director.

I knew Shiv Bosu and clearly it was not he. But I knew who it *might* be.

79

Interesting," I said. "This one we should follow."

"What if someone else comes out?"

"Can't be helped." We pulled out and followed the Mercedes.

"So many white cars," Kon observed.

"It's the right colour for this climate," I said. "Think how much heat the average black car absorbs in the sun."

Our quarry was a fast driver. We followed as he sped towards the downtown district. Kon traced our progress on a foldout map of the city that he had picked up from the bell captain at the Burj al Thani.

"We're heading west. There's a bunch of skyscrapers up ahead."

I glanced sideways at his map. "We're approaching the financial quarter."

"What's that?"

"It's what it says. Dubai aspires to become to Asia and

Africa what Switzerland is to Europe – a discreet, tax-free financial centre. So they set up this special district where corporations pay no tax. Thousands of international companies are based there, as well as the usual supporting cast of banks and attorneys."

As we approached the complex of high-rise buildings, Kon's eyes widened.

"Check out that massive tower in the middle."

"That's the Burj Khalifa, the tallest building in the world."

"I thought the Petronas Towers in Malaysia was the tallest?"

"Not anymore. You obviously don't know the story. Supposedly, the architect asked the Ruler of Dubai how high he should build it and the Sheikh said, "Just make it higher than anything else in the world." It is 2,722 feet high and has 163 stories."

"I wonder if it sways at the top?"

"Only a foot from side to side, or so they say."

The Mercedes stopped at the Burj Khalifa itself. We watched as the driver got out and handed his keys to a valet. I was sure, now, that I knew who he was.

"Look after the car," I said.

"Where are you going?"

"I'm going to follow him."

"Won't he recognise you?"

"We've never met."

"What shall I do?"

"Hang around. I'll call you."

I hastened across the forecourt to keep track of my

man. A throng of people were hurrying to work in the huge Y-shaped building and I knew that if I lost sight of him I'd never find him again. He made for the elevators. I closed to within a few feet and managed to squeeze into the same cabin before the door slid shut. There were multiple blocks of elevators; this one served only floors seventy to a hundred.

He got off at the 82nd floor. I stayed on board and pressed the button for one floor higher.

I got out at the 83rd floor and asked a young Arab in kaftan and thobe where the emergency stairs were. He eyed me oddly and pointed to a door less than six feet away. I thanked him, feigning embarrassment. "Dumb foreigner! I meant to get off on 82."

The building narrowed considerably on the upper floors. I descended the staircase, which was less elegant than the rest of the building but clean and well lit. Slit windows looked out across the roofs of lesser skyscrapers towards the sea. I don't have a great head for heights, so I only gave the view a brief glance before opening the door to the 82nd floor.

There was a small lobby with no furniture, just the doors to two suites. One bore a sign saying 'Fancy Goods Limited.' The other said 'InterOcean Bank of Dubai," in raised gold letters.

I was in the right place. This was the bank where Danie Basson had been sending the so-called architects' fees from Protea. I entered.

The suite consisted of a lounge area with sofas and glass-topped coffee tables. Panoramic windows created a spacious feeling of being suspended above the clouds. There were tellers' windows and several desks with people wearing suits.

The man I was following sat talking to a banker at one of the desks.

The young woman at a nearby desk looked at me. "Can I help you?"

"I want to open an account." I was winging it now.

"Of course." She indicated a chair and I sat.

"Can I get you something to drink?"

"Water would be nice." It would also buy me a minute to collect my thoughts. I glanced over at my man. He was almost within earshot – a few feet closer and I could have switched on my phone and recorded his conversation.

She brought my drink.

"Will that be a business account, or a personal one?"

"Business."

An account at InterOcean Bank might be useful, I thought. There was a plan at the back of my mind involving Shiv Bosu and moving large sums of money around.

She played with her computer and printed some forms for me to sign. "What about an initial deposit?" she asked.

"How about twenty thousand dollars?"

So I opened a checking account in the name of a small Panama corporation that I owned, and put twenty grand in it. I took the money from another bank account, also belonging to the Panama company but located in

Belize. How can I be bankrupt and yet have money in the bank, you ask? It's a long story. It's also one I don't want the authorities to hear, so we should probably leave matters there for now.

Meanwhile, I was glancing across at the person I came to shadow. He concluded his discussion and left as I was still signing papers.

As I got up to leave I said, "I thought I recognised that man, the one sitting over there."

"Oh, really?"

"Isn't he Basil Heinie, Finance Director of the Bosu group?"

"That's right. Do you know each other?"

I shrugged. "We've met at a few functions. Thanks so much for your help."

Smiles all round. Bank secrecy is nice but it's amazing what a casual face-to-face chat can achieve. It also doesn't hurt to splash twenty grand around. Fifty would have been even better but I didn't have that kind of money.

～

Ron Halfshaft was following the bodyguards in their truck and trying hard not to be spotted. They drove to the centre of town, parked and went into a shop.

It was a gun store. Shotguns, sporting rifles and handguns filled the window. Other items for sale included high-powered cameras and a few drones, but guns had pride of place. Ron drew to a halt and waited for the bodyguards to emerge, which they did fifteen minutes later. The taller man was carrying a package the size of a shoebox.

Ron knew nothing about guns, but the box looked like ammunition. He waited until they had driven away, then went into the shop himself.

"I'd like to buy a gun."

"What kind?"

"I'm still thinking about that. Do you sell ammunition?"

The assistant looked at him. "Do you want ammunition, or do you want a gun?"

"A gun. It's just that I saw a guy leaving here with what looked like a box of ammunition."

"That's right. It was for an AK47."

Ron knew that in the United States you could buy AK47 semi-automatic rifles capable of cutting a deer in half with a stream of bullets, in a travesty of sports hunting.

"Maybe I should get one of those."

"Well, okay, but it would be an odd place to start. If you want to get accustomed to firearms why not begin with something smaller?"

Ron let the man talk. His mind was focused on what the bodyguards might be doing that required AK47s. It worried him that they were staying at the house he might soon be breaking into. He sat up when he heard the dealer say something about a license.

"Did you say license?"

"Yes. You need a license to own a firearm in Dubai."

"But I can get that later, right?"

"I guess so. You can apply here, we have the forms."

Ron bought two small handguns and two AK47 semi-automatic rifles. Including two boxes of ammunition, he paid almost eight thousand dollars. It was the most he had ever charged on his Visa card at one time, but the transaction was approved. The assistant helped him carry his purchases to the car.

Driving back to the yacht, he felt rather odd. He was not a violent person, it wasn't his style and yet here he was, setting up a situation where he could kill people. It felt like crossing a line.

He was thinking about this when his phone rang. It was Oliver.

"I've identified the guy in the Mercedes. It's Basil Heinie, one of Shiv Bosu's henchmen. He's probably not a physical threat – he's an accountant like me and we don't do violence, at least not often. But I think we can use him to bring down Bosu."

"That's good," said Ron flatly.

"Is something the matter?"

Ron explained about his purchases.

"Well done."

"You think so?"

"You did the right thing, what can I say?"

"I'm uncomfortable about all this. I wish I had your certainty," said Ron.

"We can discuss it," said Oliver. "See you back at the boat."

80

We sat on deck looking at Ron's purchases. A pile of wrappings festooned the floor, reminding me of Christmas. On the table lay four shining weapons.

Gay came up from below. "Anyone want a drink before lunch?" She saw the weapons. "What in Heaven's name are those?"

"What do they look like?" said Ron.

"I know what guns are. We have plenty of shooting on my parents' farm in Scotland."

"You probably know more about firearms than we do," said Omar.

She shook her blonde head. "I know sporting weapons – shotguns. These are not sporting weapons."

"No," I said. "They are instruments of death. What we have to decide is whether we're willing to use them."

There was a silence.

"I say not," said Carlton. "We know more about the

people in the villa now. They are not violent as far as we know."

"Not yet," I said.

"They are protecting a very large investment," said Kon. "Who knows how far they are willing to go?"

I still had Kon's street map. I straightened it out and studied it. "It's a pity the house is not visible from the road. How can we get inside without having our heads handed to us as shish kebab?" I looked around the group. "Suggestions?"

"There may be a way," said Ron.

We looked at him.

"I think I'll go back to that gun shop."

"Not more guns, for goodness sake," said Gay.

He shook his head. "Not exactly."

∾

Ron made several more purchases. The group gathered again to see what he had bought.

The main item was a gunmetal grey device eighteen inches square and six inches high with motors at all four corners. Each motor drove a small propeller.

Carlton picked it up. "What the heck *is* this?"

Ron grinned. "It's a drone. It can hover over the villa and take photos. It will even send back video images while we're using it."

"What range does it have?" I asked.

"About a hundred yards. It has lithium polymer batteries which are the state of the art, but they limit how long it can stay aloft. A sensor monitors the charge and tells the drone when to turn round and head home. Otherwise it would run out of power and crash."

"Does that mean we can sit in the car eighty yards away and control it?" I asked.

"That's the idea."

"I like it."

~

Next morning we set out in my Infiniti, with the drone. Ron had read the manual from cover to cover and spent the evening practising. He set the controls so that the video picture came to his laptop computer.

We stopped at a safe spot and he placed the drone on a level patch of ground and pressed a key.

With a low buzz it rose smoothly into the air.

"It can go as high as 400 feet," said Ron.

"Don't waste power," I said. "Take her up to 200 feet, that's high enough not to be noticed."

We watched the screen. A clear image of the villa was displayed, growing bigger as the drone approached it. We could see the layout as if on a map. In front of the building was the pool, clear and blue.

A woman was emptying trash into bins at the back of the building. The image was sharp enough to show she had oriental features, perhaps Filipina, and was wearing a maid's uniform. She had on rubber gloves. She finished her task and went inside.

"Take the drone up to the side of the house," I said. "See if it can look in through the windows."

"Is that wise?" asked Ron. "What if they spot it?"

"We have to take the risk. Looking down on the roof won't really help us."

Ron said, "I'll do a pass at speed, along the windows at the upper front of the house. The folk inside won't spot it if we go fast enough, and if they do they may think it's a bird."

"Fine," I said. "It's worth a try."

He thought for a moment, then thumbed the remote. The drone floated to a position fifty yards beyond the eastern edge of the villa, at the height of the upstairs windows.

"We'll only get a brief glimpse of what's inside but we can replay it later at our leisure," he said. "Here goes."

As we watched our screen, the drone began its run. It accelerated and swept past the upstairs windows, so close as to almost touch them, at about thirty miles an hour. But there was enough time to see one thing that startled me – the pale face of a haggard Paul Coward peering out through a closed window.

The drone whizzed on its way, skimming the tops of the trees beyond the far end of the building.

"That's it," I told Ron. "That's enough."

"Shall I take her round and check the back of the house?"

"Not now. Let's not push our luck. Hopefully they won't have spotted it and, if Coward saw anything, he should have the sense to keep quiet."

"Whatever you say."

I nodded. "A good morning's work. Let's get back to the boat."

Guided by Ron, the drone drifted home and made a smooth four point landing a few feet from the car. Ron scooped it up and we were on our way.

~

Back on the yacht, we replayed the video. Carlton recognised Paul Coward immediately.

"The guy looks miserable," he said. "But at least he's alive. What's our next step? How do we get into the grounds?"

"Here's an off-the-wall idea," I said. "Did you see that maid putting out the trash?"

"What about her?"

"How do you think the garbage gets collected?"

Carlton shrugged. "By a garbage truck."

"Exactly."

"So?"

"The truck must come in through the gates."

"Okay, but how does that help?" Carlton sounded impatient.

"I see where he's going," said Omar. "That could be our Trojan Horse."

"Next time a garbage truck visits the house, we need to be inside," I said.

"You're dreaming," said Carlton.

I turned to Omar. "What about your friend Hassan? Would he be willing to help us out?"

"How?"

"By renting a garbage truck."

"Hassan can fix anything if the price is right."

81

Hassan the fixer got it done.

It took connections and money, a lot of money according to Hassan, but when we headed back to the villa we were in a green garbage truck, its side sporting the eagle-and-palm crest of the municipality of Dubai.

Hassan himself was driving, although we had not told him the reason for the excursion. A short, swarthy fellow with bright eyes and a ready smile, he had shown initial concern at the idea of a phony garbage run but five grand in hundred dirham notes had a calming effect and he went along with the gag.

We had checked the municipal trash schedule and luckily this was the day of the weekly collection. I held my breath as we approached the villa's grounds, but Hassan barked suitable Arabic into the microphone and the iron gate swung slowly open.

We followed the curving drive all the way round to

the back of the house where we had seen the trash bins being filled. The van stopped and Hassan got out and knocked on the back door. It was opened by the same maid.

Her smile turned to shock as Kon and I leaped out of the van and pushed our way into the house. Kon fastened her hands behind her with kitchen ties and herded her into a large closet. I heard him apologise, which did him credit, but it bothered me, this was no time for chivalry.

"She's not on our side, see that she's secured," I said.

We had a general idea of the layout of the house, from the plans on the realtor's website. We crept into the main reception room, guns ready. It was a long, handsome room, its tile floor scattered with rich woven rugs.

We had debated a lot about whether to use our weapons. To leave a pile of bodies strewn around the villa would clearly cause massive problems, but I argued that if we wanted to succeed we had to be willing to go all in.

As it turned out, the decision was taken from us. There were four men in the room – the accountant Heinie, Shiv Bosu and Shiv's two bodyguards. We tried to be silent in the kitchen but we were apparently not quiet enough because the taller bodyguard had his weapon poised and aimed in our direction.

"Drop the gun," I shouted.

He ignored me. The AK47 swung towards the centre of my body, steady and under control. I had visions of a stream of lead cutting into me.

So I shot him.

The sound was deafening. One bullet was enough. I think it hit him in the chest because he grabbed at his torso before collapsing onto a patterned Bokhara rug.

The other three offered less resistance. The shorter bodyguard had a pistol and was preparing to use it, but when we made eye contact and the muzzle of my gun centred on his stomach, he had second thoughts and lowered the weapon.

"Kick the gun over here," said Kon pleasantly. The man did so and Kon scooped it up.

Shiv Bosu's first reaction was surprise, giving way to near-fury, but he raised his hands.

His deep voice shook slightly. "What is this?"

I ignored him. Explanations later.

"Keep them covered," I told Kon. "If anyone moves, shoot him. I'm going to find Coward."

I climbed the marble stairs two at a time. The hallways upstairs were lavish and vulgar, with flowered wallpaper and a lot of gold. They looked as if they had been decorated with a view to spending as much money as possible.

The drone had shown Coward's room to be at the eastern end of the building and I made for it.

I stopped outside what I thought was the right door and tried the handle. It was locked. I put my AK47's muzzle to the keyhole and fired another shot – my second of the day. The door swung open, its frame smashed.

A shame about the woodwork, but I had a huge

feeling of success when I saw the short figure of Paul Coward. In contrast to the last time we met, he was wearing a grubby tee shirt and boxer shorts, suggesting that clean laundry was not his captors' priority. A week old beard, surprisingly grey, dusted his hollow cheeks. He smiled nervously.

"Well hello again," I said.

Downstairs, I handed Coward some yellow bag ties. "Make yourself useful," I said, indicating Heinie and the two Indians. He showed definite satisfaction as he tightened the bands round their wrists.

I nodded at Kon. "It's time to get out of here."

"What shall we do with that?" He nodded at the body on the floor.

"Take it with us, leave no traces."

"There's blood on the rug."

"Bring the rug too. Wrap the body in it."

82

We loaded our prisoners into the truck. They went in the garbage hold, not the cleanest of spaces. Kon accompanied them to keep order. The rest of us squeezed into the cabin. We made it back to the yacht without incident and loaded our cargo, alive and dead, onto Ariadne.

Omar was not overjoyed at the arrival of a dead body, but he understood the reason.

"There's a large freezer in the galley with enough room for your friend while you decide what to do with him."

That left Shiv Bosu and Gordo, the other bodyguard, as well as Heinie who seemed alert but bewildered.

"What next?" asked Carlton. He looked shaken by the violence, but resigned to the way things turned out. By now he is used to expecting the unexpected when he sends me on a project.

"We get the heck out of Dubai. But there are a couple of loose ends to take care of first."

I turned to the scowling bodyguard, Gordo.

"Here's the deal. We don't really want you around, so we're going to let you go. You have two choices. Option A: you can rat us out to the Dubai police. But then you would have to explain what you yourself are doing here, why you were armed, and so on. Which could mean serious time in a Dubai prison.

"Option B, which you may prefer, is to grab a cab to the airport, buy a ticket on the next 'plane back to Mumbai and forget the whole thing."

He frowned and looked across at the trussed Shiv who nodded grimly.

That took care of Gordo.

I turned to Hassan. "A job for you."

"Yes?"

"Pop back to the villa and let that maid out of the closet."

"Okay."

"How much will you have to pay her to keep quiet about everything?"

He thought. "Two thousand dollars."

I took out my wallet.

"Here's a thousand. Give it to her. We shall check later. If we find you gave her less we will make trouble for you."

He smiled, showing all his teeth. "I would never do such a thing."

"Good for you."

∿

That left Shiv Bosu and Basil Heinie. I had plans for both of them. But first things first. I turned to Omar.

"Time to weigh anchor."

He nodded. "The sooner we're on the high seas and away from Dubai, the better."

Later that night we tipped the body of Johan overboard in international waters, wrapped in the Bokhara rug and weighed down with a length of anchor chain.

∿

Next morning, with the sun rising over a sea as calm as Lake Okeechobee, we all had breakfast, friend and foe together.

We were out of sight of land and heading south. Neither Bosu nor Heinie knew what to expect from us, so after we had eaten I took Heinie aside and we had a private chat.

Then I assembled Bosu, Heinie, Carlton and Omar. Ron and Kon were playing video games in the rear lounge so I left them to it.

"Here's the thing, Shiv," I said, "may I call you that?"

He nodded without smiling. We had removed his handcuffs the night before but had locked him and Heinie in separate cabins. I think he finally understood that he was running out of options.

"It's time for a reckoning."

83

He scowled. "You will regret this."

"You think?"

"I am well connected in Dubai."

"Maybe so, but we have left Dubai."

I led him to the aft window of the lounge. Morning sun gleamed on the red helicopter. "Do you see that little vehicle? It can take us to any jurisdiction, including some where you have no influence at all."

"Take me wherever you like. I can afford the best lawyers."

Kon had approached and was listening. "Do you think you can buy yourself out of a murder charge?" Clearly angry, he took a step towards Bosu who flinched.

I put a hand on Kon's shoulder. "Easy."

"He's asking for it."

"I know, but he will face justice, you can rest assured."

I turned to Bosu. "By the way, here are your valuables."

He had been checked for weapons the night before with nothing found, firearms were apparently left to underlings. But there was a wallet with an Indian driver's license, some South African small change, keys on a ring with a rectangular silver charm and a wad of forty thousand UAE dirhams – ten thousand dollars. He obviously didn't like to be caught short. I looked closer at the ornament on his keychain. "What is this?"

Bosu frowned. "Nothing. A key ring."

I held it between finger and thumb, and twisted. It slid open, revealing a USB thumb drive.

I called Ron to leave his game and come and join us. I handed the drive to him. "Is this nothing?"

"No. There could be fifty gigabytes of data on that."

"What kind of data?"

"I'd have to check."

"Please do so."

Bosu looked unhappy.

Ron inserted the thumb drive into his own laptop. A table of contents appeared on the screen. I watched over his shoulder.

"Some files are encrypted," he said. "They may be tricky to open."

"Take your time."

"Here's an easy one, though. Just a line of text and a password-protected link to another page."

"What does it say?" I asked.

"Let's see." He pressed a key. "It says, 'Enter password here. Password hint: Gg@1.'"

My blood quickened. "A password, eh? What does this mean, Shiv?"

"It's private."

"Of course it is. But here's my guess. As an accountant I have to keep a lot of facts at my fingertips, but I have a rotten memory so do you know what I do?"

He scowled. "No idea."

"I write them down."

"Good for you."

"I think you do the same."

Ron was listening.

I asked him "Do you think Gg@1 is the password to a bank account?"

He shook his head. "Most banks nowadays insist on seven characters, including a numeral. Gg@1 is too short."

"Unless it's in code," I said.

A leer on Bosu's face told me I was right. The thumb drive might be the key to all his bank accounts, but the code stymied me and he knew it.

I turned to Omar. "What do you think?"

The bridge player adjusted his glasses on the end of his nose and smirked. "Ron's analysis is fine but it's like his card game – brilliant but mechanical." He nodded at Ron. "No offence."

"None taken. That's how I work."

"My approach is different," said Omar. "The four characters stand for something, right?"

Ron said, "I see no logical connection between the characters in Gg@1."

"How about an illogical connection? Something Bosu can remember but nobody else would guess. That's what a good password is, after all."

"I wonder if Bosu is a good family man?" I mused.

Omar looked at me. "Meaning?"

"Gg might stand for great grandfather or great grandmother."

Ron said, "A good thought. But he had a lot of great grandparents. Eight in fact. And we don't know their names."

That rang a bell. I was back in Joburg Casino on my only visit there, with Rebekka. I remembered the gold-framed portrait of a dignified gentleman in the lobby. "That's Vikram," she had said. "Vikram Bosu, an ancestor of the owner. The casino is dedicated to him."

"Vikram," I said to nobody in particular.

"Want me to try that?" asked Ron.

"Try vikram@1."

Ron keyed it in. Nothing happened. Omar said, "The first G in the clue was a capital letter. Try again, but with the V in vikram capitalized."

Ron did so. Immediately the screen changed. Up came ten or twelve lines of characters. Each consisted of a bank name, an account number, and an input field in which to enter another password.

Omar smiled. "We've found the keys to the kingdom."

"I wish," I said. "But I think we've still got a long way to go."

Bosu did not look upset. His lack of concern bothered me. Surely he would fear the loss of all his money. But of course, there was a second password or set of passwords. Like a safe deposit box that needed two keys.

The group dissolved, with Bosu and Heinie being taken back to their cabins and locked in.

I went to see Bosu.

"I had a chat with Basil Heinie," I said. "An interesting guy."

Bosu made a dismissive gesture. "A second rater. He does what I tell him. I doubt if he's ever had an original idea."

"You think so?"

"I know so. He's predictable, like most people who lack imagination."

"That's odd," I said, "because for a consideration he has agreed to provide me with his side of the password to each of the Bosu accounts."

It wasn't true, but Bosu didn't know that. I thought it would scare him and the look on the well fed Indian's face told me I was right.

84

G ay gave me the key to Heinie's cabin. He was
sitting gazing morosely out of the window.
"We should talk," I said.

"Yes, sir."

I took him by the arm and we went up on deck. The
weather had broken somewhat and the sun was not
scorching. We strolled the length of the boat and found a
quiet spot at the stern, disturbing a large seagull that
eyed us balefully and flapped away. Heinie kept step
with me, watching me closely, calculating, keeping his
options open, he was that kind of guy. Well I would give
him something to work with.

"I am going to break Shiv," I said. "He's trash, he
belongs behind bars."

I wasn't seeking Heinie's agreement, but I had
underestimated his sycophancy because he nodded
eagerly.

"He should be punished. My word, yes. The way he

profited at the expense of decent South Africans was criminal."

I was surprised to hear such fine sentiments from the South African, and the gusto with which he attacked his boss. I held up a hand.

"You are not blameless yourself. A lot of the money he siphoned out of South Africa over the years passed through your hands."

Heinie frowned.

"That's unfair. Those were legitimate transactions, approved by our accountants LevyTeagardenHooper. How was I to know they were the result of collaboration between the Bosus and corrupt people in government?" His eyes bulged with sincerity.

"Ah yes," I said. "Your accountants, LTH. The company that just reversed a bunch of its own audit opinions and fired three partners, right?'

"Yes, sir. Shocking!"

"But as for you, you were just following orders?"

"Exactly." He missed the irony.

"Here's the deal," I said. "It's part carrot and part stick."

"Excellent. All good deals have some of both."

"We'll see how you feel when you hear it."

"Please go on, sir!"

"First the carrot. In exchange for some co-operation in the matter of passwords, I'm going to let you keep whatever money you have saved. I suspect it's in the millions."

"Oh no, sir, I was on salary."

"Really. No bonuses?"

He went pink. "Some of my salary may have been discretionary."

"Bonuses, in other words."

He was silent. Telling nonstop lies takes energy.

"Anyway, you can keep what you have," I said. "Think yourself lucky. Now here's the stick."

I laid it out. "You can forget your project in Guinea-Malia. You will resign today."

His face fell. "Or what?"

"Or we report you and your misdeeds to everyone – the UN, the OAS, the World Bank, Protea's Police Force, the South African Revenue Service, the 'Hawks.' And, of course, the government of Guinea-Malia."

"I have friends in the administration there. The President will listen to me."

"The President has relinquished responsibility for the copper company."

"I shall deal with his successor."

"Good luck! The President has appointed his daughter, Princess Rosie, as Minister of Commerce. You've heard of her, of course. She has her father's ear."

The look on his face told me that he had. But he was not the type to give in without a struggle.

"What if I disagree? You can't force me."

"Try us. My colleague Kon would like nothing more than to insert lighted matches under your fingernails and watch you suffer."

I was slandering Kon, but he wasn't there to hear, and this was all about intimidation.

Heinie glanced round, taking in the lonely sea and the distant horizon. No comfort there. He was completely isolated and we both knew it. It didn't take him long to make up his mind.

"What do you want me to do?"

"Just co-operate in all matters involving Shiv."

I did not go into detail, it was not necessary. I knew he would agree to anything at this stage. But I added, "Nothing that will affect you adversely – I'm sure your savings are safely disposed in personal accounts."

He nodded. "It's a deal."

He seemed neither pleased nor displeased. It was pretty clear that, for him, everything was transactional – how would it affect his bank balance? It didn't make him likable, but it certainly made him predictable.

Shiv Bosu was looking dejected but I felt no pity. Whenever I was tempted to feel sorry for him I thought of the wretched housing developments in Protea.

He scowled as I entered the cabin. He was perched on the silk-covered bed eating something off a tray. The tray cloth was snowy white and the delicate china looked expensive but Shiv did not seem impressed.

"You are keeping me prisoner," he barked.

"What of it? The facilities here are pretty good."

"You know what I mean."

"I do, and it's only going to get worse for you."

I explained.

It was the financial coup-de-grace.

Back on deck Carlton said, "That stuff about carting Bosu off to another jurisdiction. That was bluff, wasn't it?"

"Was it?" I said. "It's that or return him to Dubai."

"Dubai values its good name," said Carlton. "I don't think the city fathers would cut him much slack, given the bad reputation he's acquired."

"Is there an extradition treaty between Protea and Dubai?" I asked.

"Yes. Actually the treaty is between South Africa and the United Arab Emirates of which Dubai is part. It was enacted in September 2018 so the ink is barely dry. I wonder who they had in mind?"

"So that's an option. We could get our friend Ian Smith to have Bosu indicted, federally or in Protea, for his various crimes. He would be extradited from Dubai and end up in a South African prison."

"What if he gets bail?" asked Omar.

"That's a risk, but what bothers me more is the delay," I said. "Legal processes are so slow, it could be a year before he is actually facing justice back in South Africa."

Carlton nodded. "You're probably right."

I said, "Let me think about it."

87

Well, you've cleaned me out," said Shiv later.

"Not quite," I said. "But we've made a start."

"Why not quite?"

I laughed. "You're a smart guy, Shiv. I know about your list of banks, but I suspect you still have a little something tucked away."

"I see I can't fool you, Mr. Steele, you're too clever." He smiled his ingratiating smile. It was the smile that had charmed all those politicians and civil servants. It was like spreading treacle on a hot cross bun. I let myself enjoy it for a moment, it felt pretty good.

"Where are we going now?" he asked.

"Mombasa."

He looked nonplussed. "Kenya?"

"Yes. It's a nice city with a modern airport."

"Why?"

"We're going to charter a plane and fly you back to

South Africa," I said. "I shall come too. I have a date to play squash with Rebekka Moran, although I plan to spend some time at the Country Club first. I shall play a little golf and get used to the altitude."

He scowled.

"Of course, Protea will want to talk to you about the murder of the accountant Lucy Gray," I said.

"I had nothing to do with that. It was my brother!"

So much for family loyalty. "Feel free to explain that to the authorities."

"Is there nothing I can do to make you change your mind?" His tone was pleading now.

I shook my head. "There's also the matter of funds embezzled from the affordable housing venture, not to mention that public relations contract. I'd say you're in for an interesting time."

88

S o we flew back to Johannesburg, with Bosu in handcuffs – five hours nonstop in a chartered Bombardier B-6. Kon came along as a bodyguard just in case.

Ian Smith was waiting to greet us on the tarmac with an armoured police van and escort.

He grinned. "I see you've brought me a present."

"Yep."

I went on the glass squash court with Rebekka a few days later. This time I won. I know it's only a game, but boy did that make me feel better. And she was kind enough not to hold it against me afterwards.

THE END

I hope you enjoyed *Joburg Steele*. To read more Oliver Steele, why not try one of the following:

Casino Havana

Oliver flies to Havana to save his friend Kon who has been arrested for smuggling refugees. He confronts a sadistic police chief and becomes involved in a pitched battle between Cuban soldiers and Floridian freedom fighters.

PRESS to order

Casino de France

Oliver Steele is sent to Paris to track down a nuclear terrorist who is threatening the city. He wages a battle of wits with a ruthless lawyer and the depraved but wealthy scion of an oil-rich African republic who hates Parisians and everything they stand for.

PRESS to order

Casino Qaddafi

Oliver is good at tracing missing millions but this time the funds are in Libya, a place of lethal anarchy after Qaddafi's assassination. He has to outwit hostile bankers as well as the slain dictator's murderous henchmen.

PRESS to order

. . .

It is also possible to go to my website www.grahamtem-pest.com and order from there if the links on your particular e-reader are not responsive, or if you are reading the paperback.

That's about it. I trust you are well and in good spirits, and I really hope you enjoyed reading Joburg Steele.

All the best,

Graham

ABOUT THE AUTHOR

Graham Tempest is a British-American author and optimistic golfer living in Florida.